M000197096

NEW BEGINNINGS

New Beginnings

*The story of four women
finding their future.*

Betty Mains

Charleston, SC
www.PalmettoPublishing.com

New Beginnings
Copyright © 2021 by Betty Mains

All rights reserved

No portion of this book may be reproduced, stored in a retrieval
system, or transmitted in any form by any means—electronic,
mechanical, photocopy, recording, or other—except for brief
quotations in printed reviews, without prior permission of
the author.

Paperback ISBN: 978-1-63837-855-6
eBook ISBN: 978-1-63837-856-3

CHAPTER 1

Julie

After a long, tedious drive from Connecticut to Raleigh, North Carolina, I have finally arrived. I am so anxious to get to the rental house and see what it's like. I have only seen a picture of the house, and it was impressive. I will be renting with three other women I am really nervous to meet them, wondering what they will be like. I have never lived with strangers before four women under one roof and truly hope this works out.

We have all taken jobs with the same company, Popper's, a high-end clothing manufacturer with big possibilities for a great future. The salary and benefits were too good to resist, so I decided to move here to Raleigh and start a new life. I am certain the other women also have been offered a substantial amount for them to make the move here. Eventually I'm guessing we will venture out on our own, but for this year, it is a good situation for all of us.

Popper's made a relocation arrangement with a landlord/owner of a house in Raleigh to rent to all four of us. Other than discussing the rental details on the phone, none of us have met one another. I thought this should be really interesting since we are all coming from different states and cities. It will be nice to finally meet everyone and get to know each one's background and what brought us all to the same city, working with the same company. How strange is that.?

After I was separated emotionally from my husband for some time, we finally divorced a year ago. I really needed to get out of the town where we lived with all our mutual friends around; it made it hard for me to move on with my life. It was tough ending a marriage of twenty years. Things were never that good between me and my ex. I think we just stayed together for our twins, Stephanie and Harry. One day we both finally realized there was no love or anything in common, that it was over, and we got a divorce.

Divorce is a hard decision to make, no matter what the circumstances, but it was the right thing for me to do, even though I had no idea what direction I was going to take with my life. I also had the twins, who were just about adults, and I had to deal with the disappointment they felt about their dad and I splitting up. I felt like the burden was entirely on me, of course, so I had to deal with my own emotions and my kids too. My ex and I had sold the house and split the money so we could move on with our lives. Unfortunately, that was hard on the kids, moving from the home that they had known all their lives. Stephanie and Harry had to live at my ex's place and mine, alternating weekends.

They are now turning eighteen, so they will be fine, focusing on their own lives attending college this fall and finding their future careers. Thank goodness their father agreed to pay for their college. I will be responsible for their other needs, such as clothes and books, which is fair. I will do whatever it takes for my kids' needs. They will be attending University of North Carolina at Wilmington, which will only be two hours away from me. They are going to love being near the beach, and so am I.

I am the first to arrive at the rental house, which is a beautiful big white brick colonial style with black shutters on all windows. The entire neighborhood consists of lovely large homes on an oak tree–lined street. The house has wraparound porches on the top and bottom, which will be great for the wonderful weather here in Raleigh. Outside on these porches is where I will surely spend most of my time.

I tour through the house, very pleased that it is fully furnished and has a massive kitchen with all updated appliances and a large table and stools that line the granite kitchen counter. The dining room has a beautiful blue-and-red throw rug under the table, which can seat eight people. The living room has one big sofa, a love seat, and three upholstered accent chairs. The fireplace is huge, which would be great for the winter months. It also has a den with a desk, a leather sofa, and a bathroom. There is a half bath in the hall entry, which would be great for guests. Upstairs, there were four large bedrooms and an extra guest room. There were two bathrooms at the end of each hallway. We will each have our own room and privacy, and the bedrooms are very large with big closets and also completely furnished. It is going to be a great personal space to retreat to. I love this house; it is more than what I could have expected.

Julie was unloading suitcases from her car when two cars pulled up. She waved in acknowledgment to the two girls, who got out of their cars and introduced themselves as Mary and Sandy.

"Hi, I'm Julie. It's nice to finally meet you."

They all just smiled and looked at one another, checking one another out like women do. Mary was tall and very attractive, with red curly hair. She seemed to be the type who would be a little on the reserved side—a little uptight but nice. Sandy is a very attractive blonde and is in really good shape. She was in middle thirties, medium height, and seemed very outgoing with a lot of energy. Julie thought seemed to have a sharpness about her.

Julie herself is very outgoing, with brown hair and brown eyes and in her forties, and she thought that Mary also was around fortyish.

"I just got here about ten minutes ago," Julie said, "and I toured the house. I think it is really nice. Let's go inside and see what you think."

Mary said, "If it is anything like the outside, I am going to be happy."

They walked into the house, carrying their suitcases, and looked around together.

Mary said, "I think this is really fantastic!"

Sandy added, "I don't think I will ever leave."

They all laughed. They didn't know whether to choose a bedroom or just wait for Beth. They decided to have some coffee, which they all needed after the long drives, and discovered there was at least coffee in the house until they had time to make a shopping list and stock up on groceries.

"I am from New York," Mary said, "and I will be working in the marketing department at Popper's."

Sandy said, "I am from Maryland and would be working in the IT department."

"I came from Connecticut," Julie told them, "and I always loved New England states, but the weather here in NC in September is changing me to a Southern belle." They laughed. "I will be working in human resources."

There was a knock at the door, and Beth walked in. Julie thought Beth was a lot younger with blond hair, medium build, and maybe in her early twenties. She was dressed really cute, like she just walked out of high school. She seemed really sweet but naive.

"I came from Pennsylvania, and the drive was a little longer than what I thought it would be," Beth said. "This house is awesome!"

They all had another cup of coffee and talked for a while then took their suitcases upstairs to choose rooms. Everyone quickly unpacked and added their own personal touches to their rooms to make it feel like home. They were all tired from traveling and starved, so they went out to get something to eat. They picked the Outback since they were all familiar with it, and for once, it was not crowded like it usually is, and the hostess was very Southern friendly. They each ordered a drink and talked over dinner. Everyone was a little apprehensive of how this was going to work out with all of them under one roof.

Sandy said, "I don't know what all of your situations for being here but I'm so excited to have this new job and this new beginning." They all agreed.

There was so much to talk about the drive to Raleigh, the house, and the jobs. They did not really talk too much in detail about everyone's personal background or the situations that landed them all in the same city, but that would happen soon enough. After dinner, they went to the grocery store and split the cost of groceries, and by the time they all got home, they were ready for showers and went to their rooms.

As Julie was getting ready for bed, she thought, this seems so surreal. I can't believe this is my life here in this house with three other women. After being married for so long and raising kids, I never thought I would be in this place in my life right now, but I will hopefully adjust to it all. The other girls do not have kids, so I feel a little out of place, and they may all be a little more independent than I am used to being. I have had a husband and kids that I have been taking care of for so long, and they have been my whole life. I really enjoyed being a mother, but now it is time for me and my independence.

CHAPTER 2

Mary

The whole way here from New York, I could not stop thinking about James and how convenient it was to leave him while he was out of town. This is the best move to get away from him, but I am scared and still shaking that he will find me someday. I just had no other choice really; he is very controlling and would not have left me alone if I stayed in town, so I hope I am far enough away.

There have been times when he is so hard to resist, and I still love him, which sounds crazy creepy even to myself. However, at times, things were really good. I learned those times occurred only when everything went his way. His temper had gotten to a place where I could not take it anymore. I never knew what was going to set him off or if there even was something to set him off or if he was just crazy. I could not have any friends or even spend time with family, and eventually everyone stopped coming around. I now have a chance with this job to make a new start and make new friends.

This house is beautiful; I can definitely live here. The other girls whom I am renting with are really great. I hope we can all become good friends because, Lord knows, I need some friends. It has been so lonely because other than when I went to work and saw and talked to people, I had no one. I was never able to get away from James; he was always one step behind me (or, I should say, one step in front of me) and prevented me from having a life. Now I am in my forties, and I have wasted so much of my time letting him just plain suffocate me and all my needs. I am too old to have kids now, and that really doesn't matter to me. I like kids, but it was never one of my dreams to have them.

James and I met at Starbucks one morning five years ago when he walked over and started talking to me. He told me I was beautiful and that he always had a thing for redheads. I was flattered with his charm. He always said the sweetest things to me. He looked at me with those big blue eyes, and I was hooked. It was the way he looked at me and treated me, like I was the only girl in the world, that stole my heart and made me feel very special. When a man treats you like you're the only one, then he is a unique man, and I just loved him for that until I learned his motives. We had dated about six months when he talked to me about moving in with him. I was so excited that I decided to do it. It was great having him around all the time.

We cooked together every night, our bonding time after a long day at work. Our sex life was also great, and that was another reason I stayed, but then I realized that it takes more than sex to make a happy couple, and a dominating man is just suffocating and a total turnoff. My family agreed with me that it was time to get away from him. "Take the job and don't tell him. Just leave," my mother said, and I did, with my mother helping me pack all my things.

I know I made the right decision now, and I hope he does not come looking for me and lets me move on. He knew that I was not happy with him anymore, so this should not be too much of a surprise. Being here with these girls makes me feel like I am in college again, living in a dorm but with a lot more privacy and independence, and of course, we are a lot more mature.

CHAPTER 3

Larry was not happy with me moving to Raleigh. He could not understand why I needed to take this new job that would take me away from him and to another state. I told him that it was a great opportunity for my career. "My degree is in marketing, and I am hoping that I can climb the corporate ladder fast," I told him. He said, "Take the job if that's what you want, and I will be here for you. See if you like the job, and if you don't, then please come home. I will miss you, and I will visit you as often as I can." He leaned over and kissed me, and I thanked him for being so supportive. He was so sweet about it I can't help but love him. Although he is my man, I do feel that he thinks I won't make it, will fail, and come back home. I hope not; I really need to do this right now.

Larry and I have been together since we met in college, where we both got our degrees in marketing. We never lived together. I lived at home, but we were always together when he was not working. He is successful in his job, and it takes him everywhere, and he told me that he comes to Raleigh quite often.

My family was excited for me. I am only in my twenties, so they felt that it was time to pursue my career and find my talents. They are always very encouraging to me.

When I finished college, I had applied to several positions in the Pittsburgh area but never heard from any of them. Then this job offer came, and I knew that I wanted it. The salary and benefits they offered were great for me starting out on my own for the first time. What is really nice is that I won't be alone in some apartment. I will be sharing a house with other women, and we will be sharing the rent as well. I like the idea of a house rather than an apartment, as it will seem more like home.

It is hard enough leaving home for the first time and not knowing anyone. I will miss my friends, family, and Larry, but I plan on visiting home at least on the holidays. I am young, and I want to pursue my dreams, and I want to have some fun before I settle down with Larry.

Living on my own (well, almost on my own) is going to be great, and hopefully with my new job, I will be able to get my own place eventually. I am feeling like a professional now, just like I have always hoped I would. I have finished college, and I am on my way to a career where I can actually use my degree.

My parents were both very successful lawyers who always worked hard but really liked what they did. They told me that it is important to like what you do to be happy. They have always been great parents, always there for me when I needed them. They paid for my college in full, so I don't have any debts to start out with, which is a relief. I would not have been able to make this move with a college debt. My dad even signed for my new car, which I love. It's a Subaru, so it should last a long time and will definitely make it easier driving back to Pennsylvania in the winter because it is always snowing there.

CHAPTER 4

Everything feels right. I am so glad to be here and thankful that I got this job. I love the weather here and the people I will be sharing the house with. They are all so nice. I lost my job at home, or should I just say it? I was fired. I just hate working for difficult self-serving people and wish I could be self-employed and be my own boss. I know I would be better at managing people. I am really going to have to work on starting my own business, if I could only think of what that will be and come up with the money to do it. Sometimes I feel like I am so screwed up.

I am going to miss my friends, though; we were always going out on the town together. I will have to get used to making new friends to run around with, something I never had to do; I always had friends. I dated a lot too, and some I really liked, but I haven't been serious with anybody. I just like the dating scene. I like being single and free, and I really don't want to get married since I have seen too many marriages fail. They are always happy in the beginning, but then things change. Men cheat, and women get bored with their lives, so it just does not make sense that two people think that they will always care about each other forever; it is only a fantasy. I keep myself clear of any commitment like that, and if I settle down, it will not lead to marriage, maybe just living together so I can leave if I am not happy.

The reason for my feelings is because my dad left my mother when I was young. I don't want to get married and get hurt like my mother. I watched her feel so sad for so long. She eventually remarried, but it took a long time for her pain to heal. I hated my dad for that and have never really had a close relationship with him since then. We get along, but that is about it. He left her for another woman, whom he never married, and it only lasted a year. He is still single, and I am glad he never met anyone like my mother since he does not deserve happiness. He should have appreciated what he had. The grass always looks greener on the other side, they say. However, my dad found out the hard way that it is not true. So I decided that I will depend on myself for happiness, and if anyone gets too close, I back off quickly and end the relationship; it is simply easier that way.

When I dated Glen, a guy who was so hot and a lot of fun to be with, we went swimming and boating every weekend with a group of friends, and it was a blast. He was a little too conceited and liked it when other girls flirted with him, but I did not mind since I wasn't going to stay with him anyway. He was a lot of fun and great in bed, but I knew I was moving on. There are always other guys out there to date, and I like to meet them them all and see what they have to offer.

CHAPTER 5

Julie was the first to get up Sunday morning and was feeling delighted that it was already sunny and warm, thinking it must be seventy-five degrees outside. The others got up subsequently and seemed to be well rested and refreshed after a good night's sleep, something they all needed since they arrived at the house. Over coffee, they started to talk and get to know one another a little better.

Mary said she had just ended a long-time relationship with a guy who had no intention of getting married and felt she needed to move on.

"This job opportunity was there at the right time. I was living with James at his apartment, and I had no other place to live, so this is perfect for me," Mary said.

Julie said, "I divorced a year ago after twenty years and have two grown kids, Stephanie and Harry, who are with their father right now until college begins this fall. They will be attending the University of North Carolina at Wilmington, which is two hours from here." Julie added, "I was living in my hometown in an apartment, and I liked my job with a finance firm, but I could not turn down this job offer. I needed a new start."

"Luckily, I am still single," Sandy said. "I have never married, by choice. I am thirty-five, and I like just dating. Marriage is not for me." Sandy said, "I really need this job with benefits since I was laid off from my last job." She thought, *More like fired, but I do not want to say fired since I just met these girls.* "My boss was a real son of a bitch, and I am glad to be out of there."

Beth said, "I am dating someone, but it will be long distance since he lives in Pittsburgh. I am hoping he comes here next weekend. Otherwise, it will be phone calls until he is able to come here. I am twenty-eight years old, and I needed to take this job for the experience and it was just too good to pass up." She continued. "He has a demanding job. He is getting a little tired of it. His name is Larry, and he works for a marketing firm. He has to travel a lot, and then it still doesn't stop because he is on his phone constantly doing business. He was not too happy about me taking this job here, but I had to look out for myself and my own job opportunities."

Mary asked, "Maybe he should look for another job that is less demanding?"

Beth replied, "Once I get settled, maybe he will join me here, which would really be great. He actually does come to Raleigh on business a lot, so I don't know why he could not just transfer here, but we'll see. I am hopeful."

The landlord stopped by that afternoon to make sure they all had arrived and to meet them. He asked if there was anything that they might need. His name was George; he was a middle-aged man, around fifty years old or so, with gray hair and a gray beard. They told him how happy they were with everything, and he was pleased about that. He told them a little about the area since he lived there all his life and grew up in the house. He told them to call him if there were any problems or if they needed anything.

"I will stop by from time to time, if that's okay, just to see if things need to be repaired and looked after. It is an older home, you know. Things do go wrong, so please let me know if you have any problems with anything." They all thanked him and told him they would keep his number on the refrigerator.

"That was really nice of him," Sandy said, "to be sure we are here and happy with the house. I don't know why we would not be happy. It is so perfect, and I think that showed a lot of class."

Mary said, "He probably wanted to see what kind of crazy people are living in his house." They all laughed and agreed. "After all, this place is really nice and nicely furnished, so I would be a little concerned if I were him that I rented my house out to people from out of town I did not know. I am sure he did background checks on us."

After talking and listening to the women a little more, Julie thought that the living arrangement just might work since everyone seemed really nice and cordial. They all had different personalities and ages, which made things interesting, and as long as they could get along sharing the house and paying the rent, it would be great. The setup should just be for about a year, and everyone would probably move on, get married, buy a house, find another place to rent, and so on, but right now they were under one roof, and they were going to try to make it work and live one day at a time.

CHAPTER 6

On Monday morning, Julie woke up anxious to start her new job. Everything went well that morning, she thought, with four women getting ready at the same time. They were able to have breakfast, shower, and get ready to go. After work that evening, they all met at home and decided to go out to dinner at the Outback again since it was close by, and they all loved their food. Everyone seemed stressed and tired from the first day of work, so it was nice to get out and chill together. They talked about Popper's, which was really a large place. They gave every new employee a tour, which included a library for research and a very large cafeteria, where the food was free. The conversations were mostly about everyone's jobs and getting started with all the paperwork that they had to complete before they were shown to their offices.

Julie said, "I had an advantage since I worked in finance and human resources. I knew just what to expect, and plus, I had a lot of my information sent ahead. I am not the manager but the manager's assistant. The manager, Debbie, was really nice and helpful for my first day and seemed as though she really needed my help. She was a bit overwhelmed because the company has been doing a lot of hiring. I started out reviewing all the résumés and doing background checks and reviewed all the résumés for the applicants that were being set up for interviews. It was a full day, and I really did enjoy getting right into it. Tomorrow I will be following up on the background checks and calling applicants and setting appointments for interviews. I am not sure whether I will be interviewing applicants or the manager, but it would most likely be her."

Sandy said, "I really felt confused about what they wanted me to do all day. They just left me on my own and did not introduce me to the procedures and policies of the department. I felt frustrated."

Julie said, "Maybe since it was your first day, they did not want you to get overwhelmed. See how it goes for you tomorrow." Julie added, "Sandy, you should talk to your manager, and if she does not help you, go to HR because you need to have all the policies and procedures of the company in place. Why don't you join me for lunch tomorrow? I will introduce you to Debbie, and that way, if you need to talk to her in the near future, you will at least know her, and she will know you."

"I would like that. Thanks, Julie. I will be there tomorrow."

Beth and Mary talked about their new positions. Each of them was very impressed with the company, the benefits, and the perks they offered, such as clothing discounts to the local stores, which would help with their working wardrobes.

After dinner, they drove around the city on the way back home to get a better understanding of the area and what it had to offer and to know how to get around it. There are a lot of shopping centers with small boutiques, a lot of shoe stores, and a great big mall full of well-known stores like Macy's, Belk, and Coldwater Creek, just to mention a few. Raleigh is surrounded by different subdivisions spread out and that sit back off the roads behind trees so that in most cases, you don't even know that there are homes there. Everyone was impressed with what they had seen.

"I will have to keep tabs on myself, or I will be out shopping every day with some of these stores that are available," Mary said.

Beth said, "I am so excited about being here in this fantastic city."

Beth's phone started ringing, and it was her boyfriend, Larry, telling her he might be coming to see her next weekend, and she was really happy that he was coming this soon. Mary, Sandy, and Julie decided to go out Saturday night and check out some of the nightlife in Raleigh.

Sandy said, "Raleigh is a great place to live. Do you know that it is two hours to the mountains and only two hours to the coast? I can't wait to go see the oceans and downtown Wilmington. I heard it is really pretty with lots of things to do."

Mary replied that she and her then boyfriend, James, had been to Wrightsville Beach near Wilmington a couple of times and really enjoyed the ocean and the restaurants, but they'd never really spent much time in downtown Wilmington, so it would be nice to do that.

The next day after work, Julie decided to go to the mall and get some clothes for work since all the new fall fashions were out, and she needed just about everything. As she shopped, she was excited because it was the first time she was buying for just herself. After stopping to get gas in her car, Julie headed home. When she arrived home, everyone had just finished dinner and felt bad there was nothing left for her.

"That's okay. I ate while I was out. Let me show you all my great buys!" They all had a glass of wine and chilled out for the evening.

Julie called her son and daughter to tell them about the new place and her job. She wanted to see how they were doing and if they were all set for school to start. They, at least, would know each other since they would be going to the same college, and that really made it convenient for Julie to see them. She couldn't wait to show them what she bought them for their dorms. Since their college was only two hours away instead of fourteen hours if they were still in Connecticut, she would get to see them often, especially on the weekends. Stephanie answered and said that Harry was out for the night with friends.

"I am so excited, Mom—and Harry is too—to get started with school. Dad will be driving us down from Connecticut, and he is so happy for us."

Julie told her that she was looking forward to seeing them both, and she would meet them both at the college dorms. After hanging up, she thought about how she was not looking forward to seeing their dad, but she would be civil for the kids. After all, he was their father, and that would not go away, and they wanted to keep it friendly since they did have the kids in common, the only thing. She got so angry with herself that she had stayed in that relationship so long and wasted so much time and lost so much of her.

She thought back and now see that their relationship was just not a fit for them. She was always the one to start the conversation, like he never had anything to say to her. He was a miserable person to be around. They went on a getaway trip several times, but one time in particular, he did not talk to her the whole drive home. She guessed she did not think about that time much then because she was always thinking of him and the kids. Everyone else's needs came first, and you get used to it. Thinking of seeing him when he brought the kids to college just brought it all back.

CHAPTER 7

Mary awoke suddenly to the sound of her phone ringing. Without looking at the caller ID, she answered, and it was her ex-boyfriend, James.

"Where are you?" he shouted. "Why did you leave me? I was worried about you! I called your office, and they told me you quit your job!" He had been drinking and was having a hard time talking clearly. "How could you leave me like that and not talk with me before taking off?" he asked.

"I am starting over, James. I need to be out on my own. It is over between us, and it has been for a while."

"Why don't I come to visit you so we can talk about this?" James asked.

Mary replied, "No, that won't be necessary. I left because I want to be on my own now. I need this, James. Please just leave me alone. There would be no point for you to visit me. I just got here, and I am getting settled into my job, and I am very busy."

James said, "We should keep in touch."

"Why would we do that?" Mary asked.

"I would like to keep in touch with you so that we can still be friends," James said.

Mary replied, "I don't feel that is a good idea. I think that you should just let me move on and let me have my new life. Goodbye, James."

Mary hung up the phone, thinking, *He is always so egotistical. He has to have the last say, so he was not happy that I made this decision to leave him and move away. This is hard for him to understand that I took control of myself. He will not let me get away with this. I just know it. I am so glad there are miles between us because I know this will not be the end of it. He will not leave me alone. Why did I have to fall in love with a crazy man? I feel stupid for wasting my time and not seeing the real James Brody from the beginning of our relationship. I am hoping that I can really get myself together and make a new life.*

The next morning, Mary told the other girls about the phone call from James. She did not reveal everything about their relationship because she did not want them to know how stupid she had been to be roped in by this man, but she told them that he was a jerk and about the conversation they had last night. Everyone agreed she did the right thing not letting him come to see her if she was determined to be on her own and make a new start.

Sandy said, laughing, "I am so glad that I just play the field. It is more fun that way: no commitment, just great sex."

Beth replied, "But I really miss Larry, and I am looking forward to some great sex." They all laughed. Beth said, "Really, Sandy, how many men have you been with?"

"I lost count, Beth. Just a few," Sandy replied and laughed. *She is so naive*, thought Sandy, who smiled to herself. Mary and Julie just looked at her, and Sandy thought,

They have my number all right. I can't pull anything over their eyes.

CHAPTER 8

Mary, Sandy, and Julie went out to dinner Saturday night and then planned to go to a well-known club in Raleigh and check out the nightlife. Beth's boyfriend, Larry, was coming to visit, so she was on cloud nine. Having everyone out of the house would give her and Larry some time alone. They had not seen each other for a while, so Beth was thankful to have the place to herself when he arrived. Beth and Larry had been together since college and it did seem a little strange being there without him. They did not live together, but they were always together. She thought, *I am very close to my parents and miss them too. They have always been happily married, and I want that for me and Larry.*

Beth was hoping that Larry had missed her like she missed him and that he would transfer there with his job, which would make a lot of sense. Larry always liked when she dressed sexy for him and told her she had a great body, so she was going to dress to knock his socks off tonight. They would probably go out to eat then come back and see what happened. She knew they would really enjoy each other, and she was looking forward to it.

Dinner out was a really good idea after a long week of starting a new job, getting settled in a new environment, and meeting new friends. They all needed to get out and do something different. After dinner, they went to the club, which was really big, had music playing, and had a great atmosphere. Everyone was either around the bar or dancing. They all just looked at one another, very impressed with what they saw.

Mary said, "Things have sure changed since I was free to go out on the town."

"I know. Me too," said Julie. Mary and Julie both agreed they had been living a sheltered life. Julie said, "Who knew we would be out on the town in our forties? I think that we are both still very attractive, Mary, for our age, if I say so myself."

Now Sandy, thought Julie, *is only thirty-five, never married, very pretty, blonde with a very outgoing, kind of slutty but very funny, personality. She does have a bit of a cocky attitude, which I am sure scares a lot of men off, but of course, that is my thought. I don't know about what the others think. I do think she is right, though, just play the field and be happy.*

The girls had a drink and got up and danced most of the night. "This is great! I have not danced and had so much fun for a very long time," Mary said, "and it feels good."

Sandy danced with every man who looked at her, and she was a really good dancer. Returning to the table, the girls all toasted to their new life.

Julie got up to use the restroom and was approached by a very tall, dark, and handsome guy, probably about the same age as her, fortyish. He tapped her arm and asked the crazy old line, "Do you come here often?" Julie laughed and looked at him and was caught up in his big brown eyes.

Julie said, "Honestly, I have never been here before." She smiled.

He said, "I have never been to this club either. I was just transferred here for my job."

Julie laughed again. "Yes, that is why I am here also. I just moved here for my job. I don't really get out that much. I divorced a year ago and just moved here for my job. My friends and I are out for the first time tonight, checking out the nightlife."

"My name is Ken," he said and extended his hand.

"Hi, I'm Julie."

"Can I buy you a drink?" Ken asked. He told her he divorced a year ago, and with no kids, it was an easy split. He said they both knew it was not working between them and that they had stayed together too long.

"I understand. I have two kids, so I stayed longer than I should have because of them. They will be starting college, so I guess really I don't have kids anymore, just two grown wonderful adults to be proud of."

It seemed silly, but Julie thought they connected somehow, and they were able to talk easily with each other. The conversation just flowed. They talked for a while, and then Julie invited him over to the table to meet Mary and Sandy. Knowing that he was new to this town also, Julie thought he should meet her friends. She could sense Sandy and Mary looking at them from across the room. He had a nice personality and was really kind of funny, unlike like her ex-husband, who was quiet, and she never knew what was on his mind because he never shared it with her. They never talked about their feelings or relationship, so it was no wonder their marriage did not work out after twenty years. She felt like she did not know him really, and he definitely never made her laugh.

Julie introduced Ken to her friends. "We just moved here and all share a home together and work at the same company," Julie said.

Mary and Sandy introduced themselves and seemed to really like Ken and found him interesting to talk with. Everyone danced for a while and then had another drink and ordered an appetizer, which was really needed after all the drinking. Mary said, "I am not used to all this nightlife, and I am definitely feeling the effects of the alcohol, so these appetizers were a great choice."

Sandy made everyone laugh with her sense of humor and the wild, crazy dating experiences she told them; they would make anyone blush since she did not hide any detail of her past endeavors and relationships. *Only thirty-five, but she has definitely been around,* thought Julie. Julie noticed that Mary was looking annoyed as Sandy was talking. Mary was so uptight and had a look on her face like she was an oblivious to it all as Sandy shared her stories.

Everyone talked, danced some more, and then it was time to head home. Julie could not believe the night went by so quickly and really did not want it to end.

Ken asked, "Can I call you sometime, Julie?"

"Yes, I would like that," Julie replied and gave Ken her phone number. She thought, *We have so much in common and are both new to the area. It should be interesting. He seems really nice, and yes, we have a divorce in common. He divorced a year ago just like me, and I don't really know if that is a good thing or not. Whatever! I'll take the chance. I find him very attractive, and I am liking the attention.*

While walking to the car Mary and Sandy both looked at Julie. "Julie, we can't believe you met someone tonight and gave him your phone number!" Sandy said.

"I can't believe I met someone already, and he just moved here for his job too. How absurd is that? Actually, I was only practicing because most of the time, guys never would call anyway. Maybe it was only the drinks that made him so interested in me, although I don't think he was drunk. At least I hope he wasn't." Julie laughed. "I don't know if I am making any sense right now. I had too much to drink tonight. It is always nice to meet someone and get to know them. When you move to a new area, you get a better sense of belonging."

Knowing my roommates better now, it helps a lot, so even if it does not work out between Ken and me, at least he knows all of us now as friends, thought Julie. She said, "Maybe I am drunk and should not have given him my number. Oh well, it's done now, and it does not mean I have to go out with him. Once I sober up, I may not like him at all." They all laughed.

When they arrived home, they found a note from Beth saying that she and Larry had gone to Wrightsville Beach and would be back Sunday night. "Wow!" said Mary. "The beach. That sounds really nice."

"This weather would be great for walking on the beach. I am so jealous," said Julie, and they all agreed to that and laughed.

Julie was happy to receive a call from Ken the next day. He invited her out to dinner for next Saturday. Julie was really surprised he called. Her single days were a long time ago, so she had no idea how to handle a date now. Back then there was a lot of hanging with friends and looking for a good time being single and free. They did not go out looking for that special someone at that time; they were just happy with themselves and having fun. They were mostly concerned about finishing college and moving on with their lives.

Sex was the topic most of the time, like "Should I have sex with him because I like him?" or "Should I wait and save myself for that special someone to enter my life?" Although, being naive, she found out later that everyone was having sex, but no one ever admitted it. Men would be surprised to know that women, like men, don't have to be in love to enjoy sex.

Not that she was easy, but after being with the same man for years, it would be nice to be with another man and express her sexual being again. She was really looking forward to going out with Ken; he was really nice to be around. Although she felt like she had known him and they had connected, there was more she needed to know about him. I am a little more grown up, smarter, and more cautious. *No sex first date! I know that rule!*

CHAPTER 9

Julie thought her roommates were great. Even with all their different little habits and personalities, they got along just great. They talked about their feelings and past lives. She didn't think she had ever shared so much of herself, even with her friends at home. Her job and the location of the house is just so convenient for everything. I get the feeling it was a new beginning for a new chance in life. She felt happy, happier than she had felt in a long time.

She walked into the living room, and Sandy and Mary were sitting there watching TV and looked up.

"Julie, why are you smiling from ear to ear?" Sandy asked.

"Ken called. We are going out Saturday night."

"Wow! Wow! Things are moving along," Sandy said. Sandy and Mary both smiled and were really happy for her. Sandy looked at Mary and said, "We will have to go to that club again to see if we can be so lucky."

Mary said, "I don't feel ready for anyone just yet. I am still recovering from the last loser. I really have poor judgment when it comes to men, and I just don't trust myself. I do know that I will not give anyone that much of my time again. If I meet someone, they better meet all my qualifications." We all laughed. "I know, like that is going to happen, but I would like to go out again sometime, Sandy. That was fun last night. I am a little hungover, but it was worth it, so we all need to do it again soon."

Beth walked in and said, "Hi, everyone. I am back! We had a great time. It was beautiful at the beach."

They looked at her and said, "Do not rub it in. We are jealous."

"I can't stop thinking about Larry and our relationship and what the future together is going to be. Will we make it through this long-distance relationship? I had to take this job, and I can't just sit there and depend on him. Besides, what if this relationship does not work out? I really love him, and I want things to work out because I would like to get married someday and have children with him. I am thinking truly that I took this job because I need to discover myself, and I am not quite ready to settle down, but I don't want to lose him either. Larry and I talked about this all weekend, and he is really not happy with me for taking this job, so we will see what the future holds for us," Beth said.

Mary said, "I am sure it will work out for the better."

"I am really nervous about accepting the date with Ken. I have not dated for a very long time," said Julie. "I really don't know this person, and I was so nervous when I was talking to him that I forgot to ask him where we are going for dinner."

Beth said, "You met someone and have a date?"

Mary said, "Yes, she met a guy. His name is Ken. Don't get too excited about this one date. It may not go anywhere, and I would hate to see you get hurt."

"I am aware of that, Mary, and I will keep that thought. This is just one date. I am not really looking beyond that at this time. I am not ready for marriage anytime soon." She laughed. "I am just surprised and excited that I have a date already, right now. I am feeling special."

After work on Monday, Sandy was telling them that her job was a lot better now. She had gotten the hang of it on her own, but her boss was still an ass. "She is just controlling and is jealous of everyone. She is one of those who won't let you get ahead on your job unless she wants you to. I worked for someone like that before, and I can't stand it. I am keeping my eyes open for a position to open up in another department."

Julie said, "If you have any problems, please talk to HR. That is what they are there for, and Debbie is really nice. I know she would work for you in your favor."

"I hope so," said Sandy. "I really need this job, and I can't lose it. You may be interested to know that I met this guy at work. His name is Mark, really cute, and he keeps checking me out and goes out of his way to talk to me. I'm not sure what he does there, but I am sure I will find out."

"I wonder if it is one of the guys from human resources or the business office. Does he dress in a suit or casual?" Julie asked.

"Casual. Maybe he is one of the designers," Sandy replied.

"Everyone in my department seems really content with their jobs, especially me," Beth said. "I am working toward a promotion and hope it works out that way. I know that this is a new job, and it takes time, but I want to climb the ladder fast. It's all about money, you know."

Julie thought, *How does she intend on climbing so fast? She is unrealistic and immature like I thought when I met her—no experience but wants it all.*

One evening they were all finishing dinner, and there was a knock on the door. They all looked at one another since they really didn't know anyone who would be knocking at dinnertime. Mary got up to answer it and said, "It is that time of year. It may be someone selling something."

When Mary opened the door, there was a nice-looking man standing there. "Can I help you?"

"Yes, is Beth here?" he said.

"I will get her. Beth, there is a nice-looking man here to see you!"

Beth went to the door, and she started screaming. The girls all jumped with concern; however, she was screaming with joy because it was Larry. Beth brought Larry into the kitchen and introduced him. He was tall, good looking, but seemed a little shy and nervous to meet all of them. They had already left the last time he visited, so they did not get to meet him.

Beth said, "Larry is here on business in Raleigh, and I am really surprised to see him back this soon."

Mary asked him if he would like a drink, and then they all went out onto the porch and talked for quite a while until Larry and Beth excused themselves and went upstairs to her room for the night. Julie, Sandy, and Mary finished washing the dishes and cleaned up and then decided to have another glass of wine before calling it a night.

Julie looked at Sandy and Mary and said with a laugh, "It feels really strange having a man in the house. I am not sure my kids would approve."

"It was really nice to finally meet Larry and put a face to his name. He seems very nice," Sandy said.

"He seems right for Beth," Mary said.

The next morning, Mary looked at Julie and said, "It was interesting having a man in the house, and I could hear some muffled sounds all night, and I knew what that was." They all giggled to themselves.

Sandy walked in and said, "Yes, I was jealous all night wishing, I guess, that it was me in there. Not with Larry, of course, but with someone." They all laughed. Beth and Larry were still in her room when they were leaving for work. "I don't think she is going to make it in to work today," Sandy said, giggling.

When they arrived at home that night after work, Beth was fixing them dinner. She was so awesome about doing that. "Where is Larry?" Mary asked.

"He had to leave for LA on business today, so it was a really short visit, but he will be back this weekend and stay a couple of days," Beth replied. They were happy for her. She seemed really happy and content with that.

Julie left the table and went up to take a long bath since it had been a long day. Just as she was getting in the tub, Ken called to see if they were still on for Saturday. He told her he was looking forward to seeing her. She gave him her address and asked him where they would be going on Saturday. He said he had picked out a restaurant that he heard was really nice and wanted to try it. Julie thought, *So it may just be potluck, as they say.* Julie said, "That sounds wonderful to me since I like to try new restaurants and foods."

"I will see you at 6:30 p.m.," Ken said and hung up. The thought of going out on a date with someone very attractive and nice had Julie's heart pumping. Julie got into her hot soapy bath and soaked for an hour then got into her nightgown and curled up with a book. There were times when she really enjoyed her private space and time alone.

The next morning over breakfast, Mary said, "Sandy, we should join a gym and get our bodies in shape so we can get out there and find some good, strong, good-looking men."

"Okay, I really like that plan. It relaxes me," Sandy said. "And yes, and this body does need some help. Mary, I saw there is a gym right down the street about two blocks that we could probably walk there. Let's meet there tomorrow after work and check it out."

Mary said, "I hope it is has all the latest equipment. I used to work out a lot, then of course, there was James, who wanted all my attention, so I gave it up for quite a while. It will be nice to get back into it again. Once we join, I am sure Julie and Beth will follow."

Sandy and Mary met at the gym the next day after work, and it was just what they were looking for. All the equipment was new and well laid out. They even had a juice bar, a sauna, and a walking trail around the gym. "I am impressed," said Mary, and they went and signed up immediately.

Sandy said, "I will stop at the store on the way home and will fix dinner for everyone tonight."

"Great. Thanks, Sandy." That was fine with Mary since she hated to cook. "I will tell everyone when I get home," Mary said. Everyone seemed to keep their share of cooking but her, but she would rather just help set the table and clean up.

After leaving the gym, Mary started thinking about James and what a loser he was and how he just loved himself and was always so jealous and overbearing. But she did miss being with him, and he did have a lot of charm, which was what always got her in trouble. He would just give her that look, and she would do whatever he wanted, the look that made her feel like she was his puppet. They would talk about breaking up then have sex for old times' sake, and then again she would stay with him. They really did enjoy the sex together. He was really good in bed and very attentive to her; he made her feel very special. He really scared her now, and she was glad that she was able to get away from him and move on. Why did she have to meet up with such a jerk? She guessed she was young and just did not know any better.

She hadn't told her roommates how possessive he was and how violent his temper was with her. Oh well, some things are just not worth mentioning. She felt like she was really screwed up from their relationship and should go to seek some counseling. It had been good he was far away and did not know where she lived.

Mary was entering the house when Julie pulled into the driveway, so she waited for her and walked into the house with her. "Did you work a little overtime tonight?" Mary asked.

"Yes," Julie said, "I had a lot of paperwork I did not want to face in the morning."

Beth was already home and watching TV. Mary told them both that Sandy went to the store and that she would be making dinner.

"Yay! I like that she cooks," said Julie. "I wonder where she learned to cook like she does for being so young. I will have to ask her. I personally hate to cook."

Mary said, "I cook, but it is not one of my favorite things to do."

"I like to cook," Beth said. "My mother and grand-mother taught me everything I know."

"You really are a good cook, Beth, and it is fully appreciated," Mary said. "Your family taught you well. Sandy and I joined the gym down the road. I am looking forward to getting started tomorrow after work."

"That is great," Julie said. "I should do the same and get into shape. I feel like I have put on a few pounds since

I moved here. I will look into joining. I like that it is close to home, then I just may use it."

Mary was going upstairs when her phone started ringing. She answered, and it was James. *Speak of the devil,* she thought.

"Hi, Mary. I just wondered what you are doing for Thanksgiving. I thought maybe I could come and join you," he asked.

"I don't think so, James. I am having Thanksgiving with my friends."

"What friends are you speaking of?" James snarled.

"My new friends," Mary said defiantly.

"Are they male or female friends?" Mary paused, so he asked again, "Are they male or female friends?"

"Both, James," Mary lied. She just did not want to answer his underlying question about her life right now. It was none of his business. He was just trying to see how much information about her life that he could get.

Mary said, "I just got home and have to go and get ready for dinner. Goodbye." Then she hung up. Mary realized she was almost ready to fall into his trap and ask him to Thanksgiving dinner. She needed to be careful and keep herself in line. It is really hard when you have been with someone for so long, but he would have to get used to it. She knew she had to move on. He did not know where she lived or worked, so it must've been driving him crazy. Crying, Mary thought, *What a crazy life I have lived.*

Mary walked into Julie's room as she was trying on clothes for her date this Saturday with Ken. From the clothes scattered on the bed, it looked like she did not have a clue what to wear. Mary sat on the bed and watched Julie parade in front of her with several different outfits to get her opinion.

Julie moaned, "I don't want to dress like what I wear to work. I want to dress for a date, but I am not sure how." Mary told her to try the green dress and wear a scarf with it. Julie put it on and was satisfied with how great it looked on her, so that dress was what she was wearing on her date. Now she needed the shoes, so she decided on a pair of sleek sandals. Julie confided to Mary, "I'm really not sure I want to go on this date. It was exciting at first, and now I am really nervous thinking about it, and it seems pointless. I don't really know this guy, and I don't think we will hit it off like we did that night we met. Maybe it was just the drinking."

"Go on the date, Julie. It's just a date," Mary said, "and if it does not work out, you don't have to see him again. Like you said before, this is just a stepping out for the night and feeling the freedom at last. You're not marrying him."

"You're right," Julie said.

Mary said, "It has been a long time since both of us have dated, so go and enjoy the night out."

Beth walked in the room just then. She had not heard from Larry and was getting concerned. "He is always busy, but it is not like him not to call me. It's really weird. We usually talk just about every day, and he was to be here this weekend." Mary told her that he would probably get in touch with her soon. "He is not answering his phone. It just goes to voice mail, so I don't want to keep leaving messages."

"Beth, why don't you plan on going out on Saturday night with Sandy and me if you don't hear from him? We can go to that restaurant and club again," Mary said. "That is, if you don't hear from Larry."

Beth replied, smiling, "Yes, that sounds like a great idea, rather than sitting and waiting for him to call. It will be good to get out and see this club you all have been talking about."

Sandy called out that dinner was ready. She did not disappoint them with the meal she put together. It was delicious. Sandy announced that she had been seeing Mark from work. "We have been seeing each other after work for some time now. We go to his place after work sometimes. I just thought I would share that bit of information with you about myself."

"Does that mean you won't be going out with us this Saturday?" Beth asked.

"No, I am seeing him, but that does not mean I married him. Of course, I will go Saturday night. There are always more fish in the sea, you know."

"I can't believe it," Mary said. "We just got here, and you and Julie are dating already—not that I am jealous, you understand. I am happy for you both."

CHAPTER 10

It was Saturday, and Julie was looking forward for her big night out. She showered, put on a little extra makeup, and got dressed. Looking in the mirror again, she wondered if she had put on too much makeup. Julie grinned, thinking, *I better go down with the girls and see what they think.* They were all sitting in the living room when she walked in. She knew they were hanging around to see Ken again and for Beth to meet him or to see if he showed up. They were impressed by how nice she looked in her green dress and noticed that she had put on a little extra makeup.

"Did I overdo it with the makeup?" Julie asked.

"You look just great," said Mary. She felt good and sat.

Beth said, "We are going to take a taxi tonight so we can drink and not worry about driving."

"That is a great idea. It is a better plan than we had the last time we went out. We were lucky we made it home okay," Julie said.

"I have not heard from Larry, so I guess he could not get away from his job," Beth said.

"What time are you leaving?" Julie asked. They laughed.

"We are waiting until you and your date leave."

"Oh, so you want to be here when he comes in?" said Julie. "Should I offer him a glass of wine?"

"That is a good idea," Sandy said. "We all know that he does drink. Where does he work? Do you know, Julie?"

Julie replied, "I don't know. I will have to ask him tonight. He just moved here for his job, so it must be a good one. I don't even know where he lives. I am guessing Raleigh, but I don't know. I can't believe that I am going on a date with someone that I know nothing about. If I am not back by morning, call the police." They all laughed.

The doorbell rang, and Julie got up to answer it. It was Ken.

"Hi, come on in. Would you like a glass of wine before we go?" asked Julie. "The girls are in the living room, and we thought we would all have a glass of wine—or a beer, if you prefer—before we all go out."

"Yes, I would like a glass of wine. Thank you. And it will be nice to see your friends again," Ken replied.

"They are planning on going back to the club again," Julie said. Julie and Ken walked into the kitchen, and he helped Julie pour the wine and put it on a tray for the girls. They entered the living room, and everyone said hello to Ken and started talking to him. Right away, Julie could tell it made him feel more comfortable. She thought it was really nice of them to make him feel comfortable. Ken told them that it was really nice to see them all again, and he even remembered all their names. Julie was impressed. They all talked and finished their wine.

Ken remarked that he was really enjoying living in Raleigh and that the weather was beautiful. He said, "I have met a lot of nice people at work, and they have invited me to dinner several times. It's great because it is such a transition moving to a new place. This house is really nice, and I take it you all are happy here in Raleigh."

"We are all still adjusting," Mary said, "to the new area and new jobs."

Julie thought Ken looked really handsome in his slacks and shirt, and he smelled so good too. Her heart was pounding. *I am really nervous. Maybe I was right, and we were too drunk to really like each other.*

Ken said, "I found a nice Italian restaurant that is not too far way. I hope you like Italian."

"I love Italian food. How did you know?" Julie giggled. He looked at her and smiled. She liked his smile. She was starting to feel more relaxed with him. Ken hesitated like he did not know what else to say to her, and she started to think the conversation flowed when they were drunk that night they met, so maybe it was a wrong idea to go out with him. "Where do you work?" asked Julie.

"I am an engineer for an electric company. I have worked for them for over twenty years."

"Wow, that is impressive. Not too many people can say that these days," Julie said.

"I really like what I do, and the company is great. I was sent here to run the engineering department at the local power plant and have eight people to manage," Ken said proudly.

Julie thought Ken sounded very passionate about his work; she could tell he really liked his job.

"Well," Julie said, "that is not too bad." And she laughed. "What do you think of this area?"

"I really like it, and I am still discovering all the amenities. I have not seen all there is to see yet, and I am looking forward going to mountains and the beach. Do you want to go to the beach in the winter?" Ken asked.

"Yes," Julie said, "it would be less crowded, and I love to walk the beach. It is very romantic." Julie quickly thought she should not have mentioned romantic.

When they arrived at the restaurant and were shown to their table, Ken pulled out her chair. Julie was taken by surprise because it was unexpected. They ordered dinner and just really talked a lot about themselves and got to know each other. Julie finally was able to breathe again. *He is funny when he talks about food, people, or just about anything. He can find the humor in it, and I do like that,* thought Julie.

Apparently, he was married before and had no kids, so moving here was his way of making a new start. He told Julie his divorce was not friendly. She had affairs with a couple of men, and he had caught her in bed with the last one. That was the end of his marriage.

"I guess I never really knew her," he said. "She got the house, but she also got the payments since it was not paid off. We were married fifteen years."

"That is too bad," Julie said. "I was also married twenty years and have two kids, and I am also starting over. My husband and I really never had a good relationship, and we grew apart. Like you said, I don't think I really ever knew him. He was always really quiet, and I never knew what he was thinking, and he just never opened up to me. We were like strangers to the end."

Julie told him a little about her kids and that they would be joining her for Thanksgiving. Julie said, "I have read that you should never talk about your marriage on a date, but I am glad we got it all out in the open."

"I agree," Ken said.

She talked more about her job and how she was so pleased to have found it with Popper's Manufacturing. Julie said, "I really like my house and roommates. It has been an adjustment, but already I feel that we are friends, and the house was a convenient setup for all of us to rent together. I still can't believe we are able to work together and share the rent. So far, it has worked out really well."

Ken said, "I found a real nice apartment downtown—or rather, my company found it for me after I told them what I was looking for. They put a hold on it until I was able to see it. I am happy with it. My apartment is close by. Would you like to see it and have a drink?" Julie felt so comfortable with him and wanted to see where he was living, so she agreed.

Ken and Julie arrived at his apartment building in a nice downtown area. Apparently, it was new, but with trees and bushes surrounding the building, it was very well land-scaped and looked like it had been there for years. When they entered the apartment, it was decorated tastefully with a brown leather sofa and chair, and it opened to a kitchen with granite countertops and stainless steel appliances as well as two bedrooms and a bath. It was definitely masculine in style. She could tell he was proud of it.

"I will fix us a drink, and it is one of my favorites," Ken said.

He decided that they would have a screwdriver, which Julie had had maybe once in her life, and she said, "That sounds good. I'll try one. Did you decorate the apartment yourself?" However, she knew it was too nice for a guy to do himself.

"No, I had a decorator come in and do it," Ken replied. "They were referred to me from the human resources department at work and gave me a great deal."

"They did a really nice job. I like it," Julie said, smiling.

They sat and talked about their jobs some more and how they liked it here in Raleigh and planned on staying. Julie talked more about her son and daughter, and Ken listened and seemed really interested.

"Are you enjoying the drink It is supposed to make you happy and giddy." He laughed.

"I am enjoying the drink. I have not had one of these for quite some time." Julie returned the smile. She thought, *He is just so delightful to be around. What a change from my husband. I really like being with him, and he just makes me smile.*

The evening was starting to get late, and Julie was starting to feel a little tipsy, but she did not want the night to end. She didn't feel this content too often, and it was a bit exciting and so nice to enjoy male companionship again. He leaned over to kiss her, and she kissed him back. She thought how nice it was to have him holding her and kissing her.

Then things started to heat up, and Ken tried to slide her back on the sofa. It had been such a long time since she had been with a man, and she really enjoyed the intimacy, but she was starting to feel a little uncomfortable about what was happening. No man had seen her naked body for such a long time—especially now that she was in her forties—other than her husband. Then she thought she had to stop it, and she told him to stop, but he was kissing her really passionately. She told him to stop again, and he stopped and looked at her, puzzled and a little embarrassed.

"I am sorry," Julie said. "I thought I was ready for this, but it is a bit scary to me."

Ken held her and said, "I am sorry too. I guess I got carried away."

"We are adults, but this is all new to me also, and I do apologize," Julie replied and started to cry, her head pounding. "I am not ready, and I don't put out on the first night. I am sorry if I gave you that impression coming here to your apartment."

Ken told her he was sorry again and really understood. Ken said, "I like you, and I am sorry. I thought we got along so well, but we still need to know each other better. We still have a lot to learn about each other, and we should take it slow."

Julie agreed and cried, not even understanding really why she was crying, but he held her close to him. Julie asked him to take her home.

He drove her home, and they were silent the whole time. She did not know what else to say; they said good night, and she walked in the house.

Once inside the house, Julie thought, *I don't know how I feel other than confused. I was scared being with him at his apartment alone. I should have not agreed to go to his apartment with him. No wonder he thought he could have his way with me. That was dumb. What if he did not stop? I really gave him the wrong message going there alone to his apartment with him. I guess I still have a lot to learn about being single and the dating game. I wish I would have handled the situation differently, like just saying "It's okay, let's have another drink, or "I am so tired, and I need to go home." I hope I did not turn him off from me because I really do like him. I just acted like an idiot. I really messed up my first date out and probably will never hear from him again.*

Sandy, Mary, and Beth finished dinner and went to the club to dance and have some fun and maybe find some guys. Sandy said, "Let's all order a drink, then get out on the dance floor."

"This music is so loud tonight," said Mary, "but they really play some good songs to dance to." They had a couple drinks and went to dance. Beth got back to the table from the dance floor and looked up and saw Larry across the room with another woman.

"No, I can't believe it, Larry?"

Mary looked at Beth and said, "Beth, what is the matter? You look like you have seen a ghost."

"No, no ghost. I can't catch my breath. I see Larry over there with another woman, and I can't believe it."

They all looked, and sure enough, there he was with some girl. They were hanging on each other, so it was apparently mutual affection. They were all shocked.

"What are you going to do, Beth?" Mary asked.

Beth said, "I can't believe that he comes into town, does not call me, and is here with another woman. He did not see me sitting here yet. I am going to sit here and take it all in until he finally sees me, then I am going to go over and look him square in face and tell him what a creep he is. But I may not be as nice with the words, though," fumed Beth.

They all ordered a drink and waited to see if Larry looked over. He was so into that girl that he did not look up. Beth said, "It looks like they have known each other for a while. Who is she? I just don't know what I am feeling right now, whether it's hurt, shock, or just pure anger. Maybe it is all the above."

As the waitress was bringing the drinks, Larry finally looked up and saw us all staring at him. He looked shocked and guilty! They all just sat there, and then Beth got up and walked over to him and threw a glass of wine in his face.

Larry jumped up and said, "What are you doing?"

"What are *you* doing?" Beth said. "You are an asshole, Larry. Does this, whoever she is, know about me?" Beth looked at the *girl,* who now had a smirk on her face like this was a comic scene. "Screw you both!" Beth yelled and walked away.

While Beth was walking back to the table, Larry and his whoever got up and left the restaurant. When Beth got back to the table, she started to cry and did not seem to be able to stop. Beth said, "That girl isn't that pretty, so I don't know what he sees in her, and I can't believe he is doing this to me. I wonder how he is explaining me to his date or whatever she is to him. I hope I ruined their night like they ruined mine. He looked at me like I was a stranger interrupting his dinner. That hurts the worst. I have known him forever; we have been together forever."

Mary and Sandy looked at each other, only imagining how her heart must be broken. Sandy decided to call a cab and get Beth home. Mary and Sandy were speechless. They did not know what else to say that would make a difference to help Beth tonight.

They arrived home, and Beth went straight up to her room. She was really in a bad state, which Mary and Sandy totally understood. She just did not want to talk about it anymore tonight. Mary and Sandy went into the living room, and there was Julie, sitting there, looking like she was a million miles away.

"Hi, Julie. How did your date go? Did you have a good time?" asked Mary.

Julie told them what had happend, and they were speechless.

"Are you ok?" Sandy asked. "Men, they are so unpredictable. It is easier being easy and just playing the field rather than becoming involved."

"It was not his fault, I should not have gone to his apartment. I did not handle the situation well," Julie said. "I am not involved, Sandy, it was the first date, and I am disappointed with myself, and I am confused, and I don't know if I will see him again."

Mary said, "You're not the only one that had a bad night tonight."

Mary began telling Julie what happened to Beth.

"She went to her room, really broken hearted," Sandy said.

Julie said, "I can't believe that happened to her; that is so unfair. How bold of him to come into town and do that.

I guess he did not know that he could run into her. He must think she stays at home and waits for his call, which, of course, she usually does. I think that girl must be from here, and he met her when he did business here."

Sandy said, "I bet he has seen other women all along while he was traveling, and she did not know it. She is young and really naïve."

Mary said, "But how could she have known? They have known each other for a long time. She did not deserve that. Why would she even want to think such things about him when she knew him so well or thought she did."

"Well, I am going to call it a night. I have had enough for one night myself," said Julie. "I would like to sit here and drink all night, the way I am feeling. A little disappointed, but such is life. Good night!"

Mary and Sandy just looked at each other, and Sandy said, "I told you it is easier to be single than put up with relationships. I am telling you, I have more fun."

"Sandy, please, tell me that one more time," Mary said. Sandy laughed and agreed.

"I am really getting to know Mark and enjoying my time with him."

"I'm sure you are, Sandy," Mary said and laughed. "I wish I could be like you, enjoying but not getting involved. I can learn something from you."

"Hang with me a while, Mary, and I will teach you my tricks." They both laughed and called it a night.

CHAPTER 11

"It's been a couple months already since we have been here," said Julie.

"Where has the time gone?" said Sandy.

Julie said, "It seems like we have known each other forever, and I like that, but it seems like we just got here, and Thanksgiving is just around the corner. I can't wait to see my kids and for you all to meet them. Are you going to be here?"

"I won't be going anywhere for Thanksgiving, but maybe Christmas," Mary said. Beth and Sandy both agreed they would be there for Thanksgiving too.

Sandy said, "We have a couple weeks to prepare our menu. I like a traditional turkey dinner. Why don't Beth and I do the dinner, and, Julie, you and Mary handle dessert?"

"That is a wonderful idea, Sandy. Is that okay with you, Beth?"

"Absolutely."

"Great, then Julie and I will do the desserts and the drinks," Mary said.

"Now that is settled, we can all make this a great Thanksgiving together," Julie said.

"Okay, it's Friday night. Who wants to go out for a drink after dinner?" Beth asked. They all agreed. "Although every time I go out, I fear running into Larry again. I have not heard from him at all, the bastard, not a phone call or a visit."

"Wow, the language, Beth," Mary said.

"I know, but the pain is still there. I talked to my parents and told them about Larry, and they were very disappointed that he would do that to me. I still picture the two of them sitting there together, and I just cannot get over it."

"It will get better with time," Julie said.

Thanksgiving Day finally arrived. They had all gotten up early to get the preparations going for their dinner.

"My kids are arriving around noon. They are really good kids and are doing well in school. I am so glad!" Julie said. "This will be odd for all of us being here in this house at Thanksgiving without their dad. There have been a lot of changes, but I feel they have adjusted well so far."

Julie finished breakfast and coffee and told the girls she was heading to the shower and then would come down to start setting the table. She showered and put on her green sweater and slacks and pulled out a pair of black flats that were comfortable enough to wear all day. Julie had told her kids they could stay the night, but they said they wanted to get back to study for finals that were coming up. She was a little letdown about that but so excited that they could come for the day. *It will be nice anyway,* she thought. *I just can't wait for them to see the house and meet my new friends.*

She had been so busy with her job, and they had been busy with school, studying and attending classes. They had not seen each other since school started.

Mary and Julie were both setting the table when the doorbell rang. Julie answered the door, and there was a man standing there. "I would like to see Mary," he said.

Julie called Mary, and she came to the door with a puzzled look on her face, and then her jaw dropped like she was terrified, and she said, "What are you doing here, James? And how did you find me?"

"Aren't you going to invite me in?"

"James, you should not be here. I told you that I did not want to see you."

James stepped in the door and gave Mary a frightening look or more of an intimidating look. Julie stepped back and thought, *What is going on here? Not today. My kids are coming.*

Mary said, "It's okay, James. I am just a little surprised to see you. Come in and join us if you like. You have come all this way."

When she said that, the look on James's face relaxed. "I would like that. Thank you," he said.

They walked into the kitchen, and Mary introduced everyone to James.

"Happy Thanksgiving to you, James," Sandy said. Mary asked him if she could get him some coffee.

James said, "Yes, thank you. I flew in today and thought it would be nice to see Mary and spend some time with her on Thanksgiving."

"Well, I am glad to have you here, and we will have a nice Thanksgiving with my new friends and their families," said Mary.

"Oh," he said. "Will there be others coming?"

"Yes," Julie said. "My kids are coming up from college."

Julie went to answer the door, and finally, it was her daughter and son. There were a lot of hugs and kisses; they were so happy to see one another.

"Happy Thanksgiving! Come in."

Julie introduced Harry and Stephanie to her new friends and housemates. Julie then showed them through the house, and they were really impressed.

"Mom, we can see that you are happy," said Stephanie, "and the house is beautiful."

"Thanks, Stephanie. I am happy, and I am so glad you and Harry got to meet everyone. What do you think of them?"

Harry said, "I really like them. They seem real nice, and I can tell you all get along well."

Julie said, "Let's get you a drink, and we can sit on the porch since it is a beautiful, warm day, and I will bring us some hors d'oeuvres to share until dinner is ready."

Julie spent most of the time with her kids catching up. There was so much to talk about, with them being in college on their own in a new area and far from Connecticut and their dad. Julie thought, *How nice it is to hear their stories of how they are coping with their new adventures.* She was proud to know that they have adjusted well. She told them about her new job and how much she enjoyed it. They were joined by the others and had some enjoyable conversations until dinner was ready. Later, they served dinner with a glass of wine and talked. Harry and Stephanie talked about school and their classes and new friends.

Sandy said, "Stephanie, you look a lot like your mother, and Harry, you must favor your dad?"

Harry smiled. "Yes, I do."

Mary said, "Your mother is very proud and lucky to have both of you."

Mary could not help thinking over dinner about James and what he was up to and how to get rid of him. *How did he find me? I just don't want a scene with him. He is very unpredictable in what he will do. He can be so charming and then turn into a crazed maniac.* "James, why don't we go into the kitchen and start cleaning up, and we will have a chance to talk?"

They went into the kitchen and started to clean up the dishes. *James was also so helpful in the kitchen. I guess it makes him feel macho in a strange way,* Mary thought.

He said, "I looked you up online, and that is how I found you."

She just looked at him. "Online?"

"Yes, you google a name, and it gives the address."

"That is really weird. I was going to call you so we could get together again," Mary said.

"Really, you were going to call me?" James asked.

Mary said, "I did miss you, James. I just feel we need to start our lives over separately. Things did not work out between us."

"Sex was always great, ha, you have to admit that," James said.

"But I was not happy. I was suffocating, and there is more to life than sex, James. I want you to leave soon. You are not staying here. I hope you found a place to stay."

James said, "I was hoping that I could stay with you. I may not be able to find a place, and you would not want me to be out in the cold, would you?"

"No, you cannot stay here. You will have to leave," Mary replied.

"I am not leaving," James said. "This is not resolved between us." He grabbed her arm and pushed her up against the sink and started to roughly kiss her. She pushed him away, and he pushed back, but just then Beth came walking in, and James backed off.

"I came in to put the coffee on," said Beth. "We are ready for dessert. I hope you like pumpkin pie with whip cream," said Beth.

"I will get the plates and the dessert ready," said Mary. *Again,* Mary was thinking, *this is not going to go well. What am I going to do without causing trouble on this happy Thanksgiving Day, especially in front of the girls and Julie's son and daughter? Maybe I will let him stay or help him find a place to stay and go with him. Yeah, that might work, and then I can see what is on his crazy mind.*

Beth took the coffee in a carafe into the dining room, and Mary carried the coffee cups into the dining room and went back into the kitchen.

Mary said, "James, why don't we find you a place to stay, and I will go with you for the night so we can talk? That is why I was going to call you—so that we could talk. I did feel bad about leaving the way I did. I thought we should have talked this out between us."

"Can I use your computer, and I will book a place?" James asked.

"Yes, sure. I will get it." Mary carried the dessert into the dining room, where everyone was just chatting away; it was really nice. She was glad they did not know how upset she was. Her stomach was doing flip-flops knowing that she would have to leave with James. There was no other way to get him out of this house without him making a scene.

After dessert, Julie's son and daughter left to get back to school. It would be two hours of driving for them. Julie came back in, smiling. "It was such a nice day," she said, "seeing and being with the kids. They enjoyed being here, seeing where I live, and meeting all of you. Dinner was great, and I am stuffed like the bird." They laughed, and Julie excused herself and went up to her room.

Mary said, "It is getting late. James found a place to-night, and I will be leaving with him since it has been such a long time since we have seen each other. We have a lot of catching up to do, and I will see you all tomorrow."

Mary told James she would follow him since he had a rental car, and she would need hers to get back home. He would be able to take the rental car back to the airport when he flew home. One thing she did know was that he had to leave tomorrow because he had to get back to work. She felt a sense of relief.

Beth noticed the strain on Mary's face. She thought she looked worried or stressed.

Beth looked at Sandy. "What do you think about James?"

"I don't know," Sandy said. "He seems nice and is very polite. He really seems to like Mary."

Beth said, "I walked into the kitchen, and he was kissing her, and I got the impression that she did not want him to. It was as though he was forcing himself on her. I get the impression that there was some intimidation going on. He gives me the creeps. I mean, really, she has not told us much about the relationship between them. Hopefully, I have the wrong impression, but it is a little worrisome to me."

Sandy said, "I don't know why I did not pick up on that because Mary acted very calm and cool around him. She did leave with him, so I think she is fine."

Julie walked in and said she was going to get a glass of wine. She asked if anyone wanted to join her. Sandy and Beth got a glass of wine and started talking about the day. Julie said, "I am still just so excited that I got to have some time with my kids. I know that they will feel comfortable staying here when they are able to come and visit. I am all wound up and can't relax just yet. I heard you talking about James and Mary. Is there something wrong?"

"We really don't know, Julie," Sandy said. "Beth got the impression that he seemed to be intimidating Mary."

"Intimidating and mean to Mary?" asked Julie.

"Yes, I hope I am wrong. She left with him and is spending the night with him. Let's hope she knows what she is doing," said Sandy.

"The way she hesitates talking about him sometimes makes me wonder if there were other reasons that she left him that she does not want to talk about," Julie said. "When he arrived today, Mary looked really scared when she saw him standing there, and he had a weird look on his face. I am wondering if it was an abusive relationship, and she would rather we not know about it. I have heard before that women who are abused are too embarrassed to tell anyone. The abuse goes on for years before anyone ever finds out, and sometimes it is just too late. I hope that is not the situation for Mary." They all looked concerned.

CHAPTER 12

Mary and James arrived at the hotel. "I don't know why you moved here. You need to come home, Mary," said James.

"Home? This is my home now," Mary said. "Is that why you came here, to talk me into coming back with you?"

"Yes, I want you to come back to me. I miss you very much, and I think we can work on being together," James said.

"No, I can't come back to you, so you should not have come. When you and I were together, it was me that held us together. I wanted it to go somewhere, but you did not care. It was always your way, James. I did not like the way you treated me, always being so controlling. I felt like I was suffocating. I had no friends anymore. I just could not stay with you any longer," Mary said.

"Have you been with someone else since you left me?" he asked.

"*No!* I have not," she replied.

"You're lying, and I know that you have been with someone, or you would not have left me. I know you. Who is he?"

"You know me," Mary said. "Well, James, you don't know me because after you and the way you have treated me like I was just your property, I don't need a man right now. It is nice to be me, myself, and I."

"You are full of shit. You are lying, and there is someone. That is why you moved here!" James yelled. His face turned red with anger. Mary could feel her face drain and turn white with fear. "I treated you well and loved you. I would not hurt you," James said.

"You treated me like I was a convenient whore. When I talked about marriage after all the years we were together, you just laughed and said, 'Like that would happen.' That really hurt, and you became more controlling and always aggressive toward me. James, you can't stand there and say that you love me. That kind of love I don't want. I came here for a job that I really like, if you would care to know, and I like my new home and my new friends."

"You can't live with those people forever, Mary," James said. He walked close to her and grabbed her arm and pulled her to him.

Mary yelled, "Stop, James!" as she pushed him away. "This will not work for you anymore. I refuse to be intimidated by you."

"What are you going to do?"

"I am going to leave now," Mary said firmly.

"Please, Mary," James begged. "I won't hurt you. I don't ever want to hurt you. I love you, and I want to be with you forever."

He moved over to kiss her. Mary thought, *This was the man that I liked: kind, romantic, charming.* The James that she liked could be so very, very good and also be very, very bad. She kissed him back; she was giving in. In reality, she missed him too and fell into his arms. They went over to the bed and started quickly taking each other's clothes off. She gave in to him, and they made love like they always did, with hunger and passion.

When it was over, James looked at her and said, "Has your new man made love to you like that?" She could not speak. She just glared at him.

"Oh, please, I told you I have not been with anyone. Have you been with someone, James?"

"We are talking about you, Mary," he said.

"That's right. That's the way it is. Your way, no explanation. I am leaving," Mary said. She was furious with him and herself. Mary got up and got dressed. "This was a mistake, James. I will call you, and we will talk again, but right now I have to go."

Mary walked out, scared that he would come after her and make a scene, but he did not. She drove very slowly, thinking how easy it was to get away. Usually he made a scene, yelling and getting louder when he did not get his own way. This time he did not come after her, and she hoped he would get on the plane tomorrow morning. She would be done with him. She wished she had not gone to bed with him tonight. They really had chemistry between them, and she guessed that was why he wouldn't let her go. That was why she always gave into him and regretted it later. She went home and crawled into bed, emotionally and physically exhausted.

CHAPTER 13

Julie was having her morning coffee and thinking that it had been a while since she had seen Ken. She thought, *I never did get his number, so I can't call him, but I am wondering if I overreacted to his moves and really turned him off. He probably thinks I am a psycho, but I really would like to see him again. Whatever, I guess what is done is done. I am going to start my Christmas shopping and get that done.*

Beth walked in and said, "Good morning."

Julie replied, "Good morning. The coffee is ready and hot."

"Sandy and I are going to pick out a Christmas tree and put it up this weekend."

"It's early to put up a real Christmas tree, isn't it, Beth?"

"No," she replied. "A lot of people put up a Christmas tree right after Thanksgiving."

"Well then, when I go shopping today, I will pick up the rest of the decorations for the Christmas tree."

She just looked at her and said, "Whatever." It looked like she had been crying.

"Beth, how are you doing?"

"It still hurts, Julie. I have not tried to reach him, and he has not called either. It is going to be a terrible Christmas. I thought maybe putting up our tree would perk me up."

Julie said, "I understand."

"I am going home for Christmas, Julie."

"That may help you heal, seeing your friends and family, Beth," Julie said. "I thought about going home to my parents' house, but I am going to have my son and daughter over for Christmas and celebrate right here. Beth, are you flying home, or are you going to drive?"

"I thought I would just fly home, and that will give me more time to see my parents and friends at home. I am not up to the questions about Larry yet. I know they will be asking me questions since we were always together for such a long time and especially on the holidays. We always went to the parties with each other. I think he must have been seeing that girl for a while, and he just got caught. That really hurts. You think you know someone and have a future with them, and then it's a slap in face, and you feel like nothing more than a fool."

"Beth, don't let this consume you," Julie said. "I was married, and it did not work out after twenty years and two kids, so I know how disappointed you are."

"I just never saw this coming. He really had me fooled," Beth replied. She put her head down and started to cry.

"Things will get better, and you will move on from this, with or without him. Just give it some time."

"I will. Thanks, Julie. Taking this job here was a smart move for me, or I would be still sitting there in my parents' house waiting on Larry, and he would never come."

"I know this doesn't sound right for me to say, but it is better that you found out now and did not waste any more of your time. Sometimes you only know a person by what they want you to know about them. Life is too precious," Julie said.

Julie came home from shopping, exhausted. Sandy said, "Hi, Julie. I booked my flight to go home for the holidays. I can't wait to see my family."

"That is great, Sandy! I hope you are still going to help to decorate the tree."

Sandy smiled. "Of course, I am looking forward to it. Why don't we all decorate the tree tonight after dinner, and I will fix some special holiday drink? I think we need it, especially Beth."

"Yes, you're right, Beth really has been down and needs some cheering up," Julie said. "I am so glad you and Beth like to cook and come up with these things because I never give it a thought. You're brilliant!"

"Have you heard from Ken?" Mary asked.

"No," Julie said. "He probably thinks that I am high maintenance and crazy. I should have handled the situation a little more maturely. I really blew it."

"Don't beat yourself up," Mary said before she left the room.

Julie looked at Sandy and said, "Mary has not been herself since Thanksgiving. I don't think she has heard from James, but I think that is a good thing. She is staying here for Christmas because she is worried about running into him at home."

That evening after dinner, they all finished decorating the tree and enjoyed that special holiday drink that Sandy made for them. It was a very enjoyable evening.

"The tree looks beautiful and especially with the fireplace blazing," Mary said.

"It cannot get any better than this," Beth said.

Julie said, "I always like decorating the tree. It brings me back to good Christmas memories when my kids were little and how much fun it was to see them open their presents. It also inspires me to get my Christmas shopping done." She giggled. "It's such a busy time. I am going to excuse myself and call my daughter." Then Julie's phone rang, and it was Ken.

"Hi," he said. "I hope it is okay that I called. It has been a while, and I cannot stop thinking about you but still feel a bit embarrassed about our first date and hope you can forgive me."

Julie was silent for a minute; she just did not know what to say. She was so happy he'd called, but she did not want to let him know that just yet. Julie said, "I have thought about it also, and I really feel that I may have overreacted to the situation."

Ken said, "I am so glad you have thought about it, but I really don't think you overreacted. It was so uncalled for on my part. I just really like you, Julie, and I did get carried away, and I am sorry. Can we try this again, maybe this weekend? Maybe do a dinner and a movie?"

"I would like that," Julie replied.

"Great. I will pick you up at seven on Saturday. I really look forward to seeing you again," Ken said.

"I will see you then on Saturday. Good night," Julie said.

Julie called her daughter, Stephanie, and asked her what her brother would like for Christmas. She said, "Mom, we may be going to Dad's for Christmas. He called and said since we saw you at Thanksgiving, he would like to see us at Christmas."

Julie was fuming, thinking, *How dare he do this without discussing it with me?* Julie said, "I did not know that your father had made this plan. I will need to talk to him, and maybe we can work something out. Now what does your brother want for Christmas? Are there any hints?"

After they talked for a while, Julie hung up and immediately called their father. "What are you doing? It is Christmas, and you know how I feel about Christmas with the kids. Can we work something out, maybe you see them after Christmas before New Year's?"

George replied, "That is a possibility. That way I will have more time with them."

"Okay, so will you call them and let them know the plan, George? Thank you for doing this." Julie hung up, relieved that he was nice enough to work with her.

CHAPTER 14

Ken arrived on Saturday, and Julie was really pleased to see him again. They talked on the way to the restaurant and agreed to put that one night behind them and move forward. Julie really liked that they got that out of the way because it was so awkward.

When they arrived at the seafood restaurant, it was packed with people, which usually means the food must be good. There was a twenty-minute wait for a table, so they went to the bar and ordered drinks and an appetizer. The conversation went great, and he was back to his funny ways. They talked about their Christmas shopping and plans. Ken was going to go home to his parents' house because he had not been home for a while, and his family was looking forward to seeing him. They made plans to see each other after Christmas and maybe New Year's Eve.

The movie they went to see was really good. It had romance and was also a thriller that kept them on the edge of their seats the whole time. Julie smiled to herself, thinking that the night together went well, and she missed being with him.

As they said good night and kissed, they held each other tight. Ken said, "I don't want this night to end. Let's go to the beach tomorrow since it is Sunday, and we will walk the beach and have a late lunch. What do you think about that?"

Julie said, "I love the idea. I will see you tomorrow morning then. Good night."

That following Tuesday, Sandy said she and Mark were going to go as a couple to the Christmas party. She said, "He is really nice, and we talked about meeting for lunch tomorrow. I do enjoy his company."

"Wow, that is great!" Julie said. "I have seen him around, and he seems popular around the office."

"I am not getting serious with him, Julie. You know that, don't you? I just like being with him."

"I do understand," said Julie. "The Christmas party is set up for Friday before Christmas. I don't have a date, but I am looking forward to it. I should have asked Ken, but then I thought that this is a good opportunity to enjoy hanging around the people I work with. Apparently, they are not bringing dates or husbands."

They all went shopping together one night to find dresses to wear to the Christmas party. They all needed help choosing a dress, so they thought it would be nice to use one another to critique their choices. Beth looked wonderful, no matter what she chose. Sandy really needed their help, or she would have looked like a hooker in the dress that she was going to buy, so they talked her into something else, thank goodness! It was fun, and they all found a dress and shoes. They were all set for the party.

Mary said, "I am really looking forward to the party. I am interested in this guy, Christopher. We have had lunch together, but he has not asked me out. This may give me an opportunity with him outside of work and really to get to know him better. I really do have bad taste in men."

"You have never mentioned him before," Beth said.

"I know. There is not much to say about him yet other than he is nice. I will introduce all of you to him at the party, and later you can give me your opinion of him if you don't mind."

Beth said, "You probably don't want my opinion, considering what I have been through with Larry, and I thought I knew him."

Julie said, "I guess we have all made bad choices, but how are we to really know someone?" They all agreed to that and then headed home.

The Christmas party was awesome. They had decorated the room with a huge Christmas tree and with holly all around the room. They had Christmas cactus blooming in red on all the tables, which were very pretty. The food was catered and delicious. The table had big blocks of ice sculptures made into angels, which was really creative and beautiful. There was no alcohol being served, but they had some drinks that tasted fruity and refreshing, so they did not miss the alcohol at all. Everyone mingled and talked.

Julie sat there looking and thinking she saw Sandy with Mark; they seemed to be in a deep conversation. *I am sure if Sandy could, she would be heading to bed with him, if she has not already. She does not hold back. She loves being single and loose.* Mary seemed to really get along with her fellow workers and spent a lot of time with Christopher. That was nice to see, but Beth was sulking the whole night like it hurt to be there. She was still having a hard time without Larry, and the holidays seemed to be making it worse like she was in a depression, and Julie was a little concerned for her. *I do understand what she is going through because I have been there myself, but little does she know she is better off without him. Myself, I enjoyed the music and the company of others.*

It was a great night and party. They all returned home after the party and talked about the fun they all had. Sandy, of course, did not make it home that night, and they did not even wonder where she was; they knew.

Julie was really excited getting ready for Christmas Eve. The kids would be there at any time, and she wanted everything to be perfect. She had already baked the cookies and made plenty of hors d'oeuvres and side dishes to go with the ham that was in the oven. All the gifts were wrapped and under the tree to be opened on Christmas morning. Mary helped Julie set the table and set up the drinks. Beth and Sandy had left already to go home for the holidays. The kids were going to stay a couple of nights. Julie would put her son in the den and her daughter in the guest room. They would leave the day after Christmas for their dad's.

As Julie was scanning the house to make sure everything was ready, her phone rang, and it was Ken. He called to wish her a merry Christmas and said he would see her in a couple of days. Just then, the doorbell rang. It was her son and daughter. "Merry Christmas! Ken, I have to go. My kids just arrived. See you in a couple days, and I can't wait to see you too."

The kids brought in their suitcases, and she showed them the rooms that they would be staying in. "Now let's go get ready for dinner. I know you must be starved after the drive."

Julie did not mention to the kids that she was seeing Ken because she was only dating and not sure where it would go, if anywhere. Besides, it was really their first Christmas without their dad and her together. She didn't know how they would feel about it, so she kept the conversation mostly about them and school.

The day after Christmas when they awoke, there was snow on the ground. No one knew it was supposed to snow, as it is rare in North Carolina. Julie's kids had packed up and were getting ready to go to the airport when they heard on the news that there was an ice storm predicted to get really bad. They called the airlines, and all the flights had been canceled. Julie told Stephanie and Harry to call their dad, that they would have to wait until the storm was over. *You would have thought that I had planned this delay. Yay!*

The power went out that night, and they set up candles all over the place. It looked very enchanting with the fireplace blazing. Julie thought it was really nice to have Stephanie and Harry with her for a couple more days.

Mary put out some snacks for everyone.

When the weather finally cleared up, Julie's kids left to go to their dad's and spend New Year's with him. Mary and Julie decided to go out to dinner and to the movies that night. Ken would be back from visiting his family in the middle of the week, and he and Julie were going to go to a party with some of his coworkers on New Year's Eve, which should be fun. It would be nice to see him and to meet his coworkers.

CHAPTER 15

Beth got home from visiting her family for the holidays. "I feel so much better," she said. "After talking with my family and close friends about Larry, I am coming to terms with losing him. I never thought he would do that to me, and it hurt a lot. It still bothers me that I did not know why, and he treated me so nice while behind my back he was seeing other women. My friends and family were really shocked that he would do that to me. You just feel if you know someone, you should know when they are two-facing you. Now I am moving on with my life, but my eyes are wide open from this day forward in any relationship that I have. I will never be able to feel that close bond with a man ever again. Part of me will always remember the betrayal I felt."

Mary said, "I am glad you were able to discuss it openly with your friends and family. It always helps to talk to someone who knew you both to really get the perspective of what happened. You said they were shocked too, so it was not just you that he deceived."

Ken picked up Julie, and they went for a drink so they could talk before going to the party. He told Julie how he missed her and that he was glad she was with him tonight.

She asked him if he was able to see all his family and friends, and he said he did and had a really nice time.

"Julie, I wanted to give you this," he said as he handed her a pretty Christmas wrapped present. She told him she did not get him anything. "That's okay. Just open it." She opened it, and it was her favorite perfume.

"How did you know?"

"I really like that scent on you and thought I should buy you more." She thought, *He is so sweet. He sure pulls at my heart.* They kissed.

They arrived at the party, and Ken introduced her to all his coworkers and friends and their wives. The place was decorated with silver balloons all across the ceiling, and they had flowers and noisemakers on all the tables. Julie drank a little too much and was feeling a little light-headed when the clock struck twelve. Ken moved in and hugged her tight and kissed her for a very long time. He looked at her and said, "I hope we have many more happy New Years together."

Julie just melted in his arms. *How could I be so lucky to find this man who makes me feel so loved?* Everyone yelled "Happy New Year!" and made a lot of noise with the noise-makers; it was fun. Julie had never been to a party like that, with the Southern New Year's meal served with collard greens and okra with beans and rice, a little different from pork and sauerkraut they enjoyed in the North, but really good. They had banana pudding for dessert. It was okay but not her favorite dessert. Julie was ready to go home, so they said goodbye and happy New Year to everyone and left. They arrived at her place; it was late, so he kissed her good night. They were both exhausted.

Since Sandy had gotten back from going home for Christmas, she had seen Mark several times. Sandy thought it would be awkward seeing him at work after their night out at the Christmas party because now everyone at work seemed to know that they were a couple. They were able to keep their relationship under the table, so to speak. Before, they rarely saw each other at work, only for an occasional lunch together.

She didn't like commitment, so she was just enjoying herself until the next one came along. She was not going to be taken advantage of by any man. She saw what her mother had gone through with her father. He left when she was sixteen for another woman and never looked back. Her mother picked herself up and remarried a year after her dad left, so good for her. She didn't ever want to get attached and hurt like that. Even seeing what Beth went through with Larry justified her reasoning. So she would keep her distance and keep moving on. No strings. She would make sure that she was protected.

She did not want to have kids now or maybe never. Most of her friends at home were married with kids and seemed really happy. She was happy for them, but that was not for her. Mark was very good looking. He had blond hair and big blue eyes. He was not bad in bed either, but she had had better. He really was a nice guy and a good catch for somebody else. She would continue to see him until someone else caught her eye; that was just the way she was and always would be.

Mary and Sandy went to the gym after work together. "Mary, have you heard from James?" asked Sandy.

"Yes, we have talked, but, Sandy, I don't want to see him anymore. I need to move on."

"Have you seen Christopher from work?" Sandy asked.

"No, I haven't. I don't think he was right for me."

"Why don't we go to the club after work tomorrow and see if we can pick up a couple guys?" Sandy said, laughing.

"No, Sandy, I can't just do that like you can."

"What is that supposed to mean?"

"I mean I can't just pick somebody and do what you do."

"Well, you just need to loosen up a bit. You don't know what you are missing." Mary laughed.

While they were working out, this guy came over to Mary and said he had seen her there before. He was really well built with big, muscular arms. Mary looked over at him and said, "Yes, I have seen you too." They exchanged names and talked about the gym and some of the machines that they use. "It was nice talking to you," said Mary, and she went back to working out.

Sandy walked over and said, "Now that is your chance to move in on him, Mary! Ask him out for a drink or something."

They both laughed.

"Maybe I will sometime. I think it will be best to talk to him here at the gym before venturing out with him. Like I said, I am not as adventurous as you, Sandy."

"I definitely understand that, Mary."

On Friday night, everyone was home just hanging out after a long week at work. Mary heard the doorbell and went to answer. There stood James.

"James, what are you doing?"

"Can I come in?"

"I would rather you just leave, but yes, come on in. What are you doing in Raleigh?"

"I wanted to see you."

"Can I get you a drink?"

"No, I just want to talk to you."

"Let's go in the living room and sit down."

"I cannot live without you, Mary, and I want you to come back with me."

"I am not going with you."

He grabbed Mary's arm and held it hard and said, "I am sick and tired of you rejecting me. I don't like it. You do not belong here. You belong with me. Do you hear me?"

"James, let go of my arm. You are hurting me."

He let go of her arm and tried to kiss her. She pulled away, and when she did, he smacked her across the face. She screamed for him to get out. She thought he was going to hit her again. He had those raging eyes, but Julie came walking into the room, startled.

"What's going on?"

James looked surprised. He must have thought she was home alone.

"James is leaving."

As he walked out, he said, "I am not done with you, Mary."

Mary started to cry and was shaking. Julie came over to her and asked, "What happened?"

"He has always had a temper, and he always has to have his way. He wanted me to come back to him, and I told him no, and he smacked me."

"Do you want to call the police and make assault charges against him?"

"No, he is gone now. He probably won't come back."

Julie sat there with Mary. "Mary, I did not know you have had this kind of trouble with him. You have never said anything."

"I did not want you all to know that I was with a jerk for so long. I feel so stupid. I just don't know how to stop him from showing up here. The last time I was with him, I slept with him, and that was crazy of me, but he does have that power over me. But when we left that night, I told him it was over, and he did not come after me. I thought he had changed and given up. When I talk to him on the phone, he seemed to be moving on but just wanted to talk from time to time, but now this, tonight, I am worried that he will come back."

Julie said, "If he comes back, we should call the police and maybe get a restraining order against him." They left it at that. It was up to Mary to decide if it happened again.

It was Saturday, and Mary got up early and went to the gym. It was quiet. No one was there, and it was nice to work out alone. She thought, *I really need to chill out, and this always helps. James is a piece of work. He did not want to get married after all that time we were together, but now he wants me and does not want me to have anyone else or let me move on with my life.*

She was in deep thought when Jeff came over and started talking to her. She said, "Hi, how are you today?" He answered that he was fine and was having a good workout. He asked if she would like to go out sometime. She hesitated only because right now James was driving her crazy, and she was not sure if the guy would turn out to be another thorn in her side. But she said yes anyway. There was no reason to penalize him, as he did not do anything to her.

"When you are done working out, I thought it would be nice to go get some lunch and a coffee."

"Sure, that would be nice."

They went to a deli nearby that sold sandwiches and soup and talked about themselves a little more. He had never married but dated off and on. He worked in construction, so he liked working out to keep into shape just for that. After lunch, they made a date to go to dinner and a dance on Saturday night. Mary thought, *He is not my type of a man, but it's one date. Who knows? Maybe I will learn something new about myself and dating.*

CHAPTER 16

Mark called Sandy and asked her to go out with him to a dance at the club.

"That sounds like fun."

"Okay," Mark said, "I will pick you up at eight."

Mark arrived at eight and came in to say hello to everyone before they left. Sandy thought he really was a nice guy. They went to the club downtown and danced and drank most of the night before going back to his place. They always went back to his place; it gave them a little more privacy when they did their thing together.

He put on some music and said, "Let's dance our way to the bedroom, shall we?"

They danced into the bedroom and sat on the bed. Mark lit some candles, and she helped him take his shirt off, and he started to undo her bra. She lay back on the bed while he took her clothes off, and she watched him undress. He had a great body, and she was really getting excited to have him.

Afterward, Sandy hugged him and said, "That was great!" They laughed and played some more and had another drink. Then he told her that he was thinking about accepting a new position in the company. She asked him, "What position is that?" and he said he would head the designing department. He would be in charge of carpeting and textiles.

She said, "Wow, that sounds more like a promotion."

"That is why I want to accept it. What do you think, Sandy?"

"I think, yes. It's up to you, though I am surprised you are asking me."

Mark looked at her and said, "Because I like you, and I like being with you. I am hoping that someday you will be more a part of my life and future." Sandy just looked at him, speechless.

"I don't know what to say, Mark. We will see how it goes."

Sandy was making a lot of noise in the kitchen the next day, pulling out pots and pans and grabbing at dishes. Beth walked in and said, "What are you doing making all that noise?"

"I am getting ready to cook something," Sandy said. "What does it look like?"

"Well, I am sorry I asked," Beth said and walked out.

Then Mary walked in and asked, "What's wrong, Sandy?"

"I did not mean to bark at Beth. I am just agitated this morning. Mark wants a relationship."

Mary said, "Is that a problem? I think that is great. I am happy for you, Sandy."

"*No!* Remember, I do not do relationships now, and I will have to dump Mark and move on. He is just getting a little too serious for me."

"Why don't you give it a chance, Sandy?"

"Because I don't want a relationship, and I don't give chances."

"But he is really a nice guy," Mary said.

"Well then, you can have him when I am done with him."

Julie walked in, and she had overheard the conversation and said, "I do understand, Sandy, but sometimes there may be someone who knocks you off your feet, and I think then you will go for it."

"No one will knock me off my feet, Julie, ever. I love them and leave them, remember?"

"But you should take happiness when it comes your way, even if it's not forever. I think you really like him, Sandy. That is why you are in a panic right now." Sandy gave her a dirty look.

"Oh, okay." Julie looked at Mary. "I think I will make some coffee. What are you cooking, Sandy?"

"I am going to make a pot roast for dinner tonight. If anyone will be here, you can join me." Julie and Mary just looked at each other.

"Okay," Julie said. "We'll be here." They were actually afraid to make her angry if they weren't going to be there.

"Julie, I am on my way to the gym. Why don't you join me?" Mary asked.

"I would love that, Mary. Let me get changed," Julie replied.

Ken called later that day, and Julie asked him to join them for dinner. Sandy always made more than enough, and he accepted. "I will see you at 6:00 p.m."

Dinner was great, and Ken and Julie decided to go out for a while. They ended up at his apartment and talked. They started kissing, and she really felt that she was totally ready for him now and waited for him to make a move.

They headed for his bedroom and took off their clothes. It was the first time they were intimate, and they moved slowly and enjoyed each other to the fullest. They were great together, and she felt a special bond with him that she had not felt for a long, long time.

Julie told him, "Wow! We should have done this sooner."

He said, "Well, if I would have had my way…" They both laughed.

He seemed to enjoy her body despite all her forty-some-thing flaws. She felt really sexy with him. She ended up staying the night, and they had more fun. In the morning, he brought her coffee in bed. They sat there admiring each other over coffee.

He said, "I like you a lot, and I really enjoyed last night." Julie told him she was really feeling the same and would like more of last night. He smiled. "I can definitely accommodate you. I think you are now turning into a loose woman, and I like it." They laughed.

She got up, showered, and dressed for him to take her home, reluctantly. She would rather have stayed for more.

Julie thought, *I have now turned into a slut and am liking it. I might as well enjoy it while I can.* She laughed to herself.

Back to reality, Ken dropped her off at home and took off to join his bowling league. Julie went to her room and changed her clothes before she went out to do some errands.

I think that I am really having feelings for him, and I am feeling it is too soon, or maybe it's the excitement of being with another man. It's been a long time. What do you do when it is too soon but it feels so right? I think he feels the same. Since both of us have been through divorce, we must both know that we should take it slow and not go too fast. I don't know if he is thinking of marriage again, but right now I don't know if I would want to get married again and take care of somebody else again. I have really started to enjoy this new life. I still need to talk to my kids and let them know now that I am seeing someone. I am sure I will when the time is right.

I went over and knocked on Mary's door. "Come in," said Mary.

"I just wanted to see if you're okay. I have not really talked to you since the other night privately."

"I am okay, but the jerk keeps calling and cussing me out. I stopped answering the phone, but I don't want him to show up again."

Julie said, "We will make sure that we answer the door, and we will tell him that you are not home."

"Okay, that sounds like a plan," Mary agreed. "We better tell the other girls so they know and so they don't let him in. I think it would be a while before he would be able to get away from his job, so we can all relax for now. I am so sorry and embarrassed that you had to witness my mess."

"That's okay, Mary. It is not your fault."

"I met someone today at the gym, Julie. His name is Jeff. We had lunch together after our workout today. He seems interested, but he has not asked me out yet."

"Great! I hope he does. It would be good if you would get out." Julie started to leave.

"Oh, by the way, how is Ken?"

"He is great," Julie said and smiled.

"I know that look, Julie!"

Sandy was sitting in the kitchen and said that she was going to have Mark over today and watch a movie together.

"That sounds nice, Sandy. I think you're over being upset with him."

"No, I just know it is time to move on sometime soon. He will have to get over it."

Julie said, "Are you sure you don't really like him, Sandy?"

"I like him, but you know me, moving on."

"Well, I think you two make a great couple, but that is my opinion."

Julie started thinking, *What is her problem with men? I think she has issues or something. She has never been married, so what is the deal? I will have to ask her that at some time.* She thought the place was becoming the drama house. She was starting to get a little homesick, and she should go visit her parents and see some of her old friends. She should take the kids home with her for at least a weekend. It would be a trip to Connecticut, but it would be worth it.

Her friend Diane said that she wanted to come and visit, and Julie told her that it would be wonderful. She would love to see her, so maybe she would call with a date she was coming sometime soon, probably for the weekend. Gladly they had a guest room, so she would have a room to stay. Julie can't wait for her to enjoy the weather there.

Diane had been divorced now for three years. Her kids were all grown and had jobs. It had been hard moving there in so many ways. She thought it would have been her ex George who would have moved away, not her. Her kids seemed to be adjusting well, though. College is an exciting time, getting ready for a future job and life.

Julie's mother told her she heard that George was seeing someone when she talked to her last. It felt a little weird and made her feel a little sad but good for him and the best for her. They say men get married sooner after a divorce than women. They have a better chance at that.

Julie decided to tell the kids that she was seeing someone the next time they were together just to let them know, and maybe they could meet him sometime. They were grown adults now. They might not work out, but she was enjoying it now while it was. She really enjoyed being with him; they had a lot in common. He really liked browsing antique stores with her, and they even bought a couple of things for his place. She really couldn't wait to get her own place so she could get these little things to put around.

Sandy thought things went well with having Mark over. She liked him, but she would not get involved emotionally with anyone. She didn't want to care too much about him now or in the future. She liked to detach herself from commitment.

Sandy told Mark that she wanted to see other people, and he took it well. She was surprised he told her he had the feeling that she was going to say that. He agreed that they should see other people. They both thought it would be awkward at work, but she thought it would be okay.

Sandy told Julie about Mark and her seeing other people, and Julie was a little concerned. "Sandy, why do you have this detachment about men? Did something happen that makes you not want to commit?"

Sandy told her about her parents' situation. Julie said, "Every relationship is different, and that does not mean that it will happen to you and your relationships. You should let your guard down and go with the happiness that you are feeling with that person right now."

Sandy replied, "I guess I am a very complicated person, but thanks for the advice."

Mary answered the door, and there was Jeff, right on time. He helped her to the car and opened the door for her. In the car, Mary was thinking it was difficult to make conversation since he was a bit quiet. Some men act like you know what they are thinking, or they just aren't thinking. It is so annoying. Mary had gone out a long time ago with a guy who just kept looking at her, and she kept thinking he was going to say something but never did. It was like he had a conversation with himself and thought he was sharing it with her in his mind. Of course, that did not work, and she dumped him. Jeff might turn out to be like that guy, and that meant this would not work out either.

Dinner was nice, and when they got back to the house, Jeff asked if he could see Mary again.

She thought the date was pleasant enough, so she told him to call her, and she would be seeing him at the gym sometime. *I am not really sure we have anything in common other than the gym, so I really don't think I will go out with him if he asks,* thought Mary. *I really do make terrible choices in men. I really liked Christopher from work, but he never called me for a date, and I never talked to him again since the Christmas party.*

CHAPTER 17

On Monday morning, Sandy went to the office, and there was a note from Mark. He asked her to see him for lunch today. *This may be a tough situation,* thought Sandy, *to keep my distance from him when we both work together.* She called him and told him that she had a lot of work to do today, and she would be having lunch in her office while she worked. He was a little disappointed; she could tell, and she told him they would do lunch another day.

Her boss came walking into her office and asked if she had seen her work orders. Sandy told her no as she just arrived. She said, "I want you to address that right away." *She is such an ass,* Sandy thought as she walked out. There was no good morning; just do it. She looked at the work order, and there was a department having some issues with their email accounts. She got on it right away and solved the problem.

She went on with the rest of the day and did get a lot of things accomplished. After all this time, she thought she still didn't have a connection with the staff in the department. None of them were very nice; they were just a bunch of nerds or something. She just did her job and go home. She kept thinking that there might be an opening sometime soon in another department, and if there was, she would take it. The boss came in before she left and said she did not complete her work order.

Sandy replied, "I did complete my work order and also did some extra work."

"I will not keep telling you to keep up with the workload. You missed this work order," her boss said and walked out. Sandy looked at the order, and it was the one that she did complete, so she finished up and left. When Sandy went out to her car, there was Mark standing there.

He said, "I thought maybe we could go get something to eat."

Sandy said, "Sure, Mark. Where did you want to go?"

Mark replied, "I think Mexican."

She smiled and said, "Let's go. I am having trouble with my boss. Mark, she hates me and just keeps giving me a hard time. This was good to get out with you to get my mind off it."

After dinner, they ended up at Mark's house and in bed. *I am just too easy,* thought Sandy. *I am glad I am on the pill.* Mark took her back to her car. It was late, and she drove home.

Mary hesitated but decided to go to the gym. She liked Jeff as a person but did not think it was going to work out dating him. She walked into the gym, and there he was. *Now,* Mary thought, *I have got to end this, and I need to find the*

words because he is nice, but he is just not for me. After putting up with James for so long, I just want my next love to be the right fit.

Jeff walked over and said, "Hi, how are you?"

"I am fine, thanks. Listen, Jeff, I know that we went out, and I had a really nice time, but I think that we should be friends and nothing more."

He said, "I must have done something wrong. I thought we had things in common."

Mary just looked at him and said, "No, we don't. I thought it would be the right thing to do since we come to the same gym that I should be up front with you. I don't want to lead you on like I am interested. I told you I just got out of a long relationship, and I need my space right now to know exactly what I want."

Jeff said, "I do understand, and I would like being friends with you, Mary. I will see you around." Mary felt bad; she did hurt his feelings, but it was better to get it out in the open. She walked away and continued doing her workout.

Beth told Mary and Julie that she still missed Larry, but she was definitely moving on. "I can't get over that the creep never called to say 'I am sorry,' or 'I am sorry I hurt you.' However, I don't care anymore, and I have been going out with the girls at work, and we are having a great time. We are all getting together tomorrow after work at Carly's house for pizza night. She also invited some of the guys from other departments that she knows to join us, so it will be fun and something to look forward to with mixed company in the bunch of us."

"That is the best thing to do when trying to get over someone—get out with friends," said Julie.

"That's what I try to do," said Mary. "Moving here was the first step, if he would just leave me alone. Every day I worry about him showing up."

"Well, I hope that does not happen again," Beth said.

Beth was thinking how the get-together at Carly's was really a lot of fun and how they all interacted totally with the guys from the office. Some were really funny. There were some positive sides of them they never saw in the office. When all the guys left, it was just the girls left.

Carly said, "We should plan to do this more often. What a great night! I did not think it would turn out like this. We will have to come up with excuses to have more parties, like football games, Halloween, or whatever we can come up with." They all agreed to that.

"There are definitely a couple of potentials for me that I would really like to get to know and go out with," Beth said.

Sandy had been seeing Mark for quite a while now. They never started dating anyone else, and she had never stayed with someone this long. She liked him, but she did need to break the relationship off. She didn't want to hurt him.

She had not been feeling well lately, probably because of the stress from work. Her boss was an idiot; she was always in her face about something.

When Sandy arrived at work, she was standing there again at her desk.

She came over and said, "We need to talk in my office."

Sandy followed her into her office.

"I am sorry," she said, "but you are not working out in this position, and I am going to have to let you go."

"What! You can't get rid of me. I have done nothing wrong but do my job."

"I disagree," she said. "You have not completed your work orders every day."

She looked at her and said, "You are a bitch and a liar, and I have completed all of them unless you are hiding them from me."

"Pack your stuff and get out."

"I will go to human resources and turn you in for harassing me, you creepy bitch," Sandy said.

Sandy went up to human resources crying, and Julie came over and asked what was wrong.

"I was fired," she told Julie. "That bitch just fired me, and I want to talk to Debbie."

Julie told her to have a seat. Debbie came out and called Sandy into her office. It wasn't long before Julie saw Sandy leave, crying, and just walked past her.

Julie went into Debbie's office and said, "What happened? That was my friend Sandy, Debbie."

"Well, I know, and I am sorry, Julie, but we have to let her go because she became aggressive toward her manager and called her a bitch. We cannot tolerate that behavior. She should have come to us if she was having a problem with her manager."

Julie did not know what to say, so she just went back to her desk.

When Julie arrived at home, she knocked on Sandy's door to see if she was all right.

"Come in," Sandy said.

"I am sorry this happened, Sandy. I wish you would have talked to Debbie earlier," Julie said.

"What am I going to do now? I should not have lost it with her, but it was a long time coming, and I just blew up at her…I have never done that before in my life, but I have never been treated so badly before this."

"You will find another job that will fit you better."

"Yes, I have to. I need to support myself, so I hope I can find a job and soon."

"You will, Sandy."

Sandy's phone rang, and it was Mark. Julie was sure he heard she was fired, so she left her alone and went down to the kitchen to fix dinner.

After dinner, Ken called Julie and asked if he could stop by for coffee. "I would love that. Come on over."

When Ken arrived, they went into the living room and sat with their coffee and had some cookies with it. Ken said, "I hope you don't mind me stopping by. I was seeing a client in this area, so I thought it would be nice to see you."

"Not at all. I like seeing you, and you made my day just being here."

Then he leaned over and kissed her.

"Sandy was fired from her job today and is really upset, which is understandable, but it has been stressful for me because there is nothing I could do, and I work in human resources. She called her manager a bitch, and Debbie said they will not tolerate any kind of aggression like that."

"I am sure she did not mean it. She was probably upset," Ken said. "The lady has not treated her right from the very beginning. I don't think people should be managed like that. Maybe she should talk to an attorney to see if she has some rights."

"I won't go there," said Julie, "or I could lose my job, so if you want to say something to her, you go right ahead, but don't involve me."

"I just may do that," Ken said. "I will not involve you. I just feel she may have some rights too. Maybe that manager needs to be fired for being unprofessional."

"Wow, you are really passionate about this situation. I have never seen this side of you."

"Well, I manage people, and I do know there is a right way and a wrong way. Anyway, I thought we would like to go to a movie this weekend and take in some more of those antique shops downtown, if you would like to join me."

"I would really like that. Maybe we could get a bite to eat and check out the antiques and then hit a late movie."

"Great! I will pick you up about four o'clock on Saturday."

He got up to leave and gave her a big hug and a kiss; it was so nice. Julie thought, *I really like him. I feel like I have found my soul mate. I hope. This Sunday I am going to visit the kids, and I will tell them about Ken, and hopefully they will agree to meet him sometime in the near future.*

Mary was walking out of the gym when James called. She thought about not answering but answered anyway. "What do you want, James? Why don't you just leave me alone?"

"Now that is no way to talk to an old lover, Mary," James said. "I am coming into town this weekend, and I would like to take you out so we can talk."

"I think I am all talked out, James. It is time for you to move on. There are other women out there that you could find to haunt."

Mary hung up the phone and walked to her car. She headed home feeling upset about the call. *Why does he not just give up on me and find someone else he can torment?* she thought.

CHAPTER 18

Sandy was so upset when she left the doctor's office. *Pregnant! I can't be pregnant! I am not married. I don't have a job,* she thought, *and I don't know what I am going do with a baby.* She cried all the way home and went straight to her room. Mark called, but Sandy did not answer the phone. She was too upset to talk to him. *What will I say to him right now? I am three months pregnant and did not know. How could I not know? Oh hi, Mark, you are going to be a dad. I hope he is really into me because he is going to be a dad, and I am going to be a mother. I thought this is just weird that this is happening to me. This can't be happening!*

Sandy came out of her room and went looking for Julie, Mary, and Beth, anybody that she could tell.

Julie was sitting in the living room when Sandy walked in. "I am pregnant!"

Julie looked up and said, "What? Did you just say you're pregnant?" Then she smiled. "You're pregnant, Sandy?"

"Yes," Sandy said. "I am going to lose my mind. I really don't know what to do. I don't have a job yet, and I have to tell Mark he is going to be a dad, and that could make him run far away. He has been very supportive to me since

I lost my job, but I don't know if he wants to be a dad, for goodness' sakes."

"When did you find out, Sandy?"

"Today! And Mark called, and I did not answer. I don't know what to say."

Julie looked at her and said, "Call him. Have him come over and talk to him in person. Once you get that out, you will know what his feelings are about this situation and then go from there. Please don't put it off, Sandy. It's only going to make you stress about it anyway. Mark is the father. He needs to know."

Sandy said, "I don't have a choice. This is his baby too. I will call him and ask him to come over tonight, and we can go in the den and talk—or in my room. I need to do this."

"You're doing the right thing, Sandy," Julie said.

It wasn't long before Mark came over. Sandy paced the floor until the doorbell rang. She was feeling nauseous and upset but led him into the den and closed the door.

"Is there something wrong, Sandy?" Mark asked, with a questioning look on his face.

"We need to talk. I have something to tell you."

He looks a little worried, thought Sandy, *but wait until I tell him the news.* "I am pregnant!"

"What?" Mark said. "You're pregnant? Oh wow!" He had a big smile on his face, and he came over and gave Sandy a big hug and said, "I thought you were going to break up with me again. This is great news, Sandy. You are having our baby."

"Mark, will you be willing to help me? I don't have a job, and in a few months, I won't have anywhere to live."

Mark looked at Sandy and said, "I want to marry you. We can plan a wedding, and you can move in with me."

Sandy said, "I thought you would run out the door."

"No, I will not run away from you, Sandy. I am here for both of us."

"This is a lot for me to take in right now. Let's talk tomorrow," Sandy said. "Let's not make a commitment that we can't keep. I am glad this happened with you. I don't know anyone that could be a better father."

He moved in close and kissed her and said, "I love you!"

"It has been a long, stressful day, but I am glad I have you."

Sandy went into the living room and started watching TV. Beth and Mary walked in and said they had just seen Mark leaving with a big smile on his face. However, Sandy seemed preoccupied about something.

Julie walked in and said, "Beth and Mary are worried about you. Did you want to talk?"

Sandy looked at Beth and Mary and said, "I am pregnant!"

"Wow! Congratulations!" they said. "When did this happen?"

"I just found out today. I have not been feeling well, and I thought it was stress. The doctor did a pregnancy test, and yes, I am pregnant. Mark was just over, and he has offered to marry me and let me move in with him. He is being so supportive of me. He said he would take care of me and the baby, that he makes enough to support all three of us. It was just wonderful. I have never felt a bond like that with anyone. He is really the best of the best. But should I marry him under the circumstances? I feel that I am trapping him into marrying me."

"Well, that is not true, Sandy. He had a place in this too, if you know what I mean."

Mary said, "I can tell that he really adores you, and I think he got what he wanted—you. Beth and I agree this is going to work out for you and for your baby."

"Well, I am going up to my room and try to sleep. This day has been just too much for me."

After she left, they all looked at one another, and Mary said, "I hate to bring this up, but what are we going to do about the rent? Are we three going to have to put in the difference?"

"I think so," said Julie. "It is too late to get anyone else to rent for a few months. I have not even thought about where I will be going or if we can rent this house for another year. Have you thought about what you are going to do?"

Mary said, "I really have not, but since you put it that way, I think we better figure something out for ourselves."

Beth said, "I don't have anywhere to go at this time. Maybe I can get an apartment."

"Well, for right now," said Julie, "we have all become such good friends. I hate to see the future coming. I think we better think about Sandy and a wedding coming up and a baby. That is a wonderful thing."

"I am so happy for her," Beth said, "and now I want to look further into the future and go back to school. I thought maybe I will do it online. I feel that I am not going to get anywhere fast at work unless I get my master's degree."

"That would be great, Beth," Julie said. "When are you going to look into this?"

"I am going over to the university here in Raleigh after work tomorrow and talk to them about how I get started. Also, when I was out with my friends from work the other day, I met someone. His name is Randy, and he is taking me out this weekend."

"Good for you, Beth! You are moving on, and that is a good thing," Mary said. Beth had never heard from Larry again.

Beth went to the university after work and talked to the admissions lady, who told Beth that she could start at any time if she was going to take the courses online. She said, "You can come in one night a week or on Saturday." Beth left and was really excited about her new future endeavors. Now she could think about her date this weekend. Randy seemed to be a nice guy to go out with. She was also thinking about looking into apartments to see what was out there to rent and the cost.

Beth's phone rang. Without looking at the caller, she answered, "Hello," and it was Larry.

"Beth, don't hang up. I want to talk to you a minute."

"What do you want, Larry, after all this time?"

"I would like to meet up with you for coffee. I am in town and would just like to talk. Will you meet me?"

"Why? Did it not work out with that other girl?" There was silence on the other end. "Okay, call me when you are in town, and I will try to meet with you." She hung up the phone.

She thought, *How weird is that? After all this time, he wants to see me. Like I care anymore. I would never give him a chance to hurt me again, but I will meet with him and hear what he has to say just out of curiosity.*

Sandy and Mark got together over the weekend and started making plans for their situation with the baby. Sandy said, "How do I know that you are not marrying me for the baby? I don't want to trap you into settling down with me."

Mark said, "I have been in love with you from the first time I saw you at work. I wanted you to be mine, and, Sandy, I hope you have feelings for me."

Sandy said, "I do have feelings for you. I just never thought of settling down with someone like this, being pregnant...I am a little scared. Are we doing the right thing getting married? Maybe we could just raise the baby together."

"We can move forward, Sandy," Mark said. "I think we will be great together. I am not planning on letting you get away from me. This is my chance to keep you forever."

They gave each other a long embrace.

Sandy said, "Then I think we should start making plans."

They both realized that they had to tell their families and get to meet all of them. They planned for the next weekend to see Sandy's mother first. Then they would meet Mark's parents the following weekend. "I know my mother is going to like you, and I hope she does not get into wedding plans," Sandy said. "I think we should just go to a small chapel and get married and have a small party with our friends."

Mark replied, "That is okay with me as long as you don't regret it later."

"I won't regret it later, Mark. I never wanted a big wedding and all that fu-fu," Sandy said. "After we meet our parents, then we can move in together. That will let us get used to each other and just be the two of us before we become mommy and daddy."

"Agreed," Mark said. "Let's get this going with our parents. I am so excited to have you move in with me. I am sure we can talk our parents into coming here for our little ceremony."

Mary was in the kitchen when Sandy and Mark walked in to tell her their plans. "Good for you two. I am glad you were able to come up with this in such a short time," said Mary.

"Well, with a baby coming, we are both on the same page and would like to be settled together before he or she is born," Sandy said.

"That is so sweet," Mary said.

Mark said, "Why don't we all go out for dinner tonight? My treat."

"Let's go!" said Mary.

They went to a local Mexican restaurant, and it was packed, but they were seated very quickly.

Mary said, "Let's have a margarita to celebrate your new life together."

"Thank you, Mary," Sandy said, "but I just realized that I can't drink anymore."

"Reality is setting in fast with me," Mark said. "Then I will not drink either. We will do this together."

Mary said, "Well then, now I feel guilty, but I am still going to enjoy a margarita myself." They laughed. After dinner, they all went home.

Sandy came into Julie's room and told her the plans that she and Mark had made.

"I am really happy for you. I knew everything would work out between the two of you."

"Julie, I am still scared that we are rushing into this, but then I feel that it is going to work out. We just need to get past what everyone thinks. I am worried about my family and what they will think, but we are grown adults, so it really does not make a difference."

Julie said, "It does not make sense that you are worrying about that stuff. Just go with what is working for the two of you, and that is the best start for a relationship. The girls and I are going to plan a wedding party for you later and a baby shower when you get back from meeting all the parents."

"Thank you! You are a wonderful person, and you have been a great friend to me. I am really going to miss living here with all of you, and I feel bad I can't help pay the rent."

"That is the last thing you should be worrying about right now. We will work things out. There is no time to get another roommate, so we will all be paying the difference. So there, we have it all worked out. Don't even think about it. You have enough on your plate right now."

"Thanks, Julie. I will thank Mary and Beth too when I see them. You are all great!"

Sandy went to Mark's place when he got home from work. They toured his condo that he bought a couple of years ago to see how all three would fit. It was a really modest condo with three bedrooms, a kitchen, a living room, and a dining room, and it had a nice screened-in back porch with a small yard. The one bedroom that was the smallest would be for the baby.

Mark said, "We can paint that now and get the baby furniture set up in there, and it will be ready for the baby."

Sandy said, "That sounds great, but we need to shop for a few things. I think it may be too early to buy all that stuff. We won't know if it is a boy or girl for a month or more."

"We could paint it in neutral colors," Mark said.

"I think we should wait until we know the sex of the baby," Sandy said.

Mark noticed when she said it that her tone was a bit snappy. Sandy still had concerns about settling down with one man; it just was not in her cards. Though she really did like Mark, she was not sure if it was love, but the situation needed it to be for them and the baby.

Mark was looking at her, thinking, *She is still unsure of me and the situation, but in time I know she will love me.* He said, "The third bedroom we will keep as a guest room for when your mother and my parents come to visit."

"That would be wonderful," Sandy said. "My mother said she would come and help us after the baby is born."

The wedding Mark and Sandy planned was at a small chapel in downtown Raleigh. It was all they wanted. Their parents came, and even Sandy's dad attended. It was a small wedding with all the people who were important to Mark and Sandy.

Julie looked at Mary and said, "They will be starting a new life together—and a family on the way. Wow! How things change so fast. I don't know how this will work out for Ken and me. We get along well, but I really don't see us getting married anytime soon. I am not sure that I want to get married again. Maybe things can stay as they are now forever."

Mary looked at Julie and laughed. "You never can tell. That just might happen, Julie."

All three girls would be able to keep paying the rent without Sandy, so they notified the landlord and took her name off the lease. They had been talking with one another about their plans on what they would do when the lease was up and considered talking to the landlord to sign a lease for another year. That was something they must decide before it was too late and he found other renters to move in.

The summers here in North Carolina do get awfully hot. It must be in the low hundreds, thought Mary as she was leaving work. She could not wait to get into the car and put the air-conditioning on. She decided and made an appointment to have a facial and get her hair done at a local spa instead of going home.

She was thinking about what her future was going to be. Sandy was married and having a baby, Beth was starting school again, Julie was happy with Ken, and here she was. What would she do? Most of all, where would she live? She had better start thinking about buying a house or maybe renting an apartment. She really liked it there. The weather was hot at times, but most of the time, it was really nice compared with Maryland. The people were nice too. Even at her workplace, there were nice, ambitious people. Maybe she should look into buying a townhouse. That way, it would have little maintenance to care for. She thought she could handle a townhouse, but she was not sure if she could care for a big house. James was right, she couldn't live with these people forever.

Beth was cooking something in the kitchen when Mary and Julie walked in. She liked to cook too when she was anxious about something.

"Beth, how is it going with you and Randy? Are you still seeing him?" Mary asked.

"Yes, we go out often when he is not working out of town. You won't believe who called me the other night."

"Who?" asked Julie.

"Larry called me. He wants to see me and talk after all this time, and I am wondering why. I am so over him, but I agreed to meet with him sometime when he is in town. He probably broke up with that girl and now wants to start seeing me again, which is ridiculous if he thinks I would ever consider going back with him," Beth said.

"I would let him have an earful...," Mary said.

"It is your time to give him the 'You did me wrong and it is unacceptable' speech," Julie said.

"Yes, that is what I plan. I just hope that I see him squirm like a rat. I am going to fix myself up and look really good. I want him to regret even more of what he is missing out on."

"I like that," said Mary.

"Have you heard from James again?" Beth asked.

"No, and that is a good thing. Finally, he gave up, and I don't ever want to see him again."

Mary said, "I am going to go work out and do a little shopping."

Beth just sat there thinking of what she could wear for her little meeting with Larry; it was her plan to execute. I just want to hear what he has to say.

CHAPTER 19

Julie called Ken. "Let's go to the beach this weekend. I need to get away."

"Great idea, Julie. Let's leave Friday after work and come back on Sunday. Which beach are you thinking about going to?"

"I thought we would go to Wrightsville Beach. It is closer, and we can come back even late Sunday. I will call and set up the reservations."

"I am looking forward to getting away with you and cheering you up," said Ken. "See you Friday after work! I will pick you up, and we will be on our way to a beach weekend, and don't forget to pack your bikini." Julie laughed.

After she hung up, she thought, It is a getaway, and I have told the kids about Ken. It would be a good time to have dinner together so they can meet Ken. I hope he does not get offended since I did say getaway, but this will just be for Saturday evening dinner, and since we are that close, I want to see the kids. I really need this with all the drama at home.

On Friday, Ken picked Julie up. While they were on their way to the beach, Julie said, "Ken, I just wanted to tell you this is a getaway for us, but I do want you to meet my kids since were are so close to their university."

"I would be happy to meet Stephanie and Harry. Why don't we take them to dinner tomorrow night?"

"I am glad you said that." Julie laughed. "That is what I had planned. I know they will be happy to meet you, and I know that they will like you."

They arrived at the beach and unpacked in their gorgeous beach house overlooking the beach, which they found online. They got into their suits and immediately went to the beach. It was after 6:00 p.m., and the beach was just about deserted, so they sat and stared out to the ocean. The sun was starting to set, and it looked so pretty and very romantic. Julie always loved staring at the ocean and walking the beach. It helped her feel peace inside.

When they got back to the hotel from the beach, she called the kids and told them they would like to meet them tomorrow for dinner. They were really excited about it, so she felt the meeting with Ken would go well.

Ken and Julie got up the next day and made love. It was wonderful. They ordered breakfast from room service with champagne and went to the beach for the day. It was hot, and the ocean water was warm and clear. They sat and read and would go in the water periodically then come back out and read some more.

The day went fast, and it was time to get ready for dinner. They told the kids to meet them at a known seafood restaurant, Bluewater, which they were familiar with. When they arrived, Stephanie and Harry were already there. Julie introduced Ken to them, and they looked pleased with him. They were taken to their table and sat, and right away Ken asked Harry how his summer classes were going and asked Stephanie how she enjoyed taking extra classes. It seemed like they all got along well, so Julie was very relieved.

When they left, Ken said, "You really have a nice family. You did a good job in raising them. They are so easy to talk with." Ken and Julie enjoyed the rest of their getaway together then headed back on Sunday after stopping at the many shops.

CHAPTER 20

Julie went to her room and called her daughter to see what she and her brother thought about Ken. Stephanie said she was excited for her and told her that she and Harry both really liked Ken. She also told her that she knew that her father was seeing someone. Friends told her about it months ago. Julie was shocked. She never even gave it a thought that they would hear it from someone other than her. She guessed she goofed on that one, but she did not seem to care in the least about it. Stephanie also shared that she was seeing someone from school and they had gone out several times. Julie was pleased for her and told her that she was so glad that she was seeing someone.

After she talked to Stephanie, Julie called Harry to tell him how nice it was to see him and get his feedback personally about Ken. Harry told her that he was really happy for her and that he really liked Ken and that they made a nice couple. That made her feel really good that both her kids were happy for her and were truly sincere and both really liked Ken. That would make the relationship a lot more enjoyable for her.

Mary got a call from James and thought, *What is this? Beth gets a call from Larry, and now James is calling me.* She let the call go to her voice mail and ignored it. She was on her way home from work and decided to go shopping for some new clothes and shoes. Maybe that would cheer her up. She was thinking all day how she was going to get on with her life once they all moved out of the house. *Although we still will see each other at work, it is going to be different living alone again. It has been a long time since I have lived by myself. I really do not have many new friends or old friends, thanks to James and how he was always dominating my life.*

When she returned home and went up to her room, she decided to listen to her voice mail. James said that he was coming into town and wanted to see her and to give him a call back. She did not call him back. She didn't know what to say to him other than "Do not come here, and leave me alone." She got a bubble bath and went to bed. She was so down and out. She did not see or talk to anyone.

Julie met Mary in the kitchen, and Mary asked how her weekend went. Julie could tell Mary did not seem to be herself, but she said she had a good time. "How was your weekend, Mary?"

"It was fine. I just relaxed and went shopping for some clothes and shoes. I will show you after work tonight. Beth left for work already, but she said she will be making dinner tonight, so I will see you then."

Mary got to work and was busy all day. It seemed to take her mind off things with her life sitting on the edge.

She really felt like she was depressed with decisions in her life that always seemed to go so wrong. *I still have months yet to worry about where I am going to live, but I feel we just got here, and it is time to go already.* The day went by really fast, and she headed home.

Beth was to make dinner tonight for everyone, so that was a relief. Maybe she would go home and do some online shopping for an apartment or house. Mary said, "It just seems like everything is moving so fast. Sandy got married and having a baby, and all of us need to find a place to live right now. It is just too much for me to take in. Also, James keeps calling me and wants to come this weekend to talk. I don't know how to handle him and just wish he would give it up."

Mary walked out of the room feeling that she did not want to share anything more with her friends. Beth and Julie continued fixing dinner.

CHAPTER 21

Mary was walking out of work on Monday when she was approached by a man. A coworker was watching from the window in the office. The man approached Mary, and they seemed to be arguing, and then the man walked to his car like he was leaving, and Mary started walking to her car. Then the man pulled a gun out of his car, turned around, and shot Mary in the back twice. He walked back to his car and left.

The coworker screamed and called out to her other coworkers, "Call 9-1-1! Mary has been shot in the parking lot!" She ran to help Mary. She was able to get his license plate number as he was leaving.

The ambulance arrived and took Mary to the local hospital, where she died minutes after arriving at the emergency room. Sally, the lady who had seen it all, notified Julie and Beth. They arrived at the hospital but was too late. Mary was already gone. They could not believe it happened and to their dear friend. She was dead. They both broke down and cried, holding each other for support. With tears in her eyes, Julie asked who did it and why.

Julie looked at Beth. "We have to call Sandy and Mark and let them know what happened to Mary." The doctor said the hospital would be notifying the family. "When her family comes up, they can stay with us. This is just awful." As they left the hospital, Julie told Beth it had to be James. "She was so intimidated by him and said he was calling her continuously and would not leave her alone."

"We need to go to the police with this information," Beth said. "Mary told me he was in town this weekend and wanted to meet with her, but she never answered his call, which may have set him off to do such a thing."

"Poor Mary. How sad. I just can't believe this happened. I have never experienced anything like this in my life," Julie said. "Mary was such a good person and friend."

When they got home from the police department, Sandy and Mark were there at the house waiting for them. They all cried and held one another, wanting the pain of losing a friend to go away. They told Sandy and Mark that when they were at the police department, the police told them that Sally, Mary's coworker, saw everything, and with her quick response to Mary, she was able to get the license number and identified James Brody. "He was arrested for murder in the next county."

"I am so relieved they got him so he can't hurt anyone else, but I wish we would have known it was this bad so we could have saved Mary," Julie said.

The funeral was two days later. They all attended, along with family, friends, and some of Mary's coworkers, including Sally. She told them that she wished she could have done something to help her; it was a horrible thing to witness, and it happened so fast.

Beth's meeting with Larry was delayed due to Mary's funeral. Beth really did not want to see him; she was still grieving over Mary, but she went anyway. Beth dressed to kill and had her nails and hair done so that she would be perfect for this meeting. They met for lunch at a quiet café downtown not far from her company. She walked in and saw that Larry was sitting in a booth. He looked up at her, and she could tell by the look on his face that he was very pleased by how she looked. He looked good too, and he got up to welcome her. They sat and looked at each other.

Beth said, "What did you want to talk to me about, Larry?"

"I wanted to tell you that I was stupid and am so sorry for what I did to you. I am young, and I guess I just wanted to see what else is out there, but there is no one that would be better than you, and I know that now. Please forgive me. I would like for us to work this out and get back together, Beth."

Beth looked at him and said, "I would never consider going back with you. I would never trust you again, and I have moved on with my life and am back in school. I am dating again, and I am very happy. You did me a favor, Larry. I feel that this happened to set me free for a new life of contentment and happiness. So if I would not have discovered your deceit, I would still be living with your lies. It was nice seeing you, Larry. Have a good life."

Beth got up and walked out. Beth could feel his eyes on her back and really wanted to look back to see his face, but she did not want to give him the benefit of having her look at him. Beth went back to work and told her friends how it went, and they were proud of her for standing her ground with Larry.

"We all know that you will be better off without him," they said, and Beth agreed.

CHAPTER 22

That Saturday, Beth got up, and Julie was sitting in the kitchen drinking coffee.

"Hi," said Beth.

Julie looked up like she was deep in thought. "Hi, Beth. I was just sitting here thinking how so much has happened and wondering where to go from here." Julie began to cry.

"I know," said Beth. "We have not had much time to talk because of everything that has happened. I don't want to sound selfish thinking about what we are going to do now about our rent. I don't know how you and I can afford it. I was sitting here wondering if we talk to the landlord, maybe he can reduce the rent so that you and I can stay here for another year or maybe find another roommate or two to help with the rent. Our lease is up in September, and I don't know who we would find to lease with us for a couple months."

Julie said, "I like your plan. Let's talk to the landlord. If he agrees, maybe we can afford to stay for another year. Let's see if we can meet up with him today."

The landlord agreed to stop over. Beth and Julie told him about everything that had happened, and he knew, of course. He had agreed to let them sign another lease and reduced the rent for them so that they could stay.

"What a relief," Julie said. "He was really considerate to us. That definitely buys us some time, Beth, so we can figure out our next step of our new lives."

"Randy and I are going out tonight. Would you and Ken like to join us?"

"That would be nice. Maybe we can see a movie or something to get our minds off of things."

"We were actually planning on seeing a play downtown and then going to dinner at a famous steakhouse."

"That sounds like a good time! I will call Ken."

Ken agreed, and they all went out at seven to see the play. The play was delightful to see. Afterward, they went to the restaurant and talked all evening; it was really fun.

Randy seemed really nice, and Julie was happy for Beth because she really needed someone like him to get her to move ahead. Randy said he worked for an IT company at Research Triangle and had been there for five years. He was interesting. He liked to go boating and fishing and went to the beach a lot in Wrightsville Beach because it is only a couple of hours away. Julie told him that her kids were going to a school in Wilmington, and he said that was where he went to school and found a job at his IT company.

When they left the restaurant, Julie told Beth, "We should have Ken and Randy over for barbecue sometime soon and invite Mark and Sandy and some friends. It would be nice to do something different."

Beth and Julie went over to see Mark and Sandy's place. It had been a while since they had seen them. "I hope things are working out for the two of them," said Julie.

"Me too," Beth said. "I can't wait to see their place since they decorated the nursery."

When they arrived, Mark answered the door, and Sandy was setting out some appetizers and iced tea. The place was very nice with plenty of room for a new family. Julie said, "This was just too big for one single guy anyway, so it is great you two moved in. How are you feeling, Sandy? You are really starting to show. You are about seven months now, right?"

"Yes, I am feeling great, and I love eating for two. Mark said I eat enough for the three of us."

Sandy showed them where the nursery was set up for the baby. They had it all planned out and seemed to be getting along beautifully. Mark was a godsend for Sandy, and Julie was pleased at how nice it had turned out knowing how Sandy went kicking and screaming into a relationship. Julie thought, they really did love each other.

As they were leaving, Julie told them, "We are having a barbecue next Saturday. We would love you to come and invite friends if you would like. We invited everyone for six o'clock."

"It still feels like home to me, so we would be delighted to come over Saturday for the barbecue," Sandy said.

"Sandy, everything is taken care of with the landlord. I thought you would be pleased to hear that."

"I am so glad. I was feeling a little guilty about moving out and leaving you with the high rent. What happened to Mary was awful, and I still can't get over it that she is really gone."

"We all feel the same way," said Beth.

Julie got home that night and thought about calling her kids to invite them up for the barbecue too. That way, they could bring a friend and stay all night if they wanted to because there was plenty of room for them. Julie told Beth her plan.

Beth said, "Yes, that would be fine. I may even invite some of my friends from work. It will be fun."

So they sat and made a shopping list and plans for next Saturday. They decided to have a firepit with some chairs around it in the backyard; they thought everyone would enjoy that. They really needed it. Since Mary died, they all had been living in grieving motion. It had been over a couple of months now, and when a friend is taken away, it feels so unreal like there is a part of you missing. It was such a freaky thing that happened and affected them all. They had packed all of Mary's things and sent them to her family. They cleaned and redecorated the room, and it was so hard to have to do those things.

Julie called her kids and told them the plan for Saturday and asked if they would like to come to their cookout. They were excited and said they would be happy to come, and she told them each to bring a friend.

Julie was getting ready for work the next day. It was a lot easier for some reason, maybe because they were able to move on despite what had happened to Mary.

When Julie got home from work that night, her friend Diane called. She wanted to come for a visit the following weekend. Julie told her she would be delighted to have her. She could stay the week if she would like, and she could take vacation from work. She said she would only be able to come on Thursday and would head back on Sunday. Julie couldn't wait for her to see the house and where she was living now. Maybe she could talk her into moving there.

Ken and Julie had been together for over nine months now, and it seemed like they had always been together. She was looking forward to Diane meeting him. She thought she would really like him too.

Ken called her to meet him after work today. They were going to meet at the Italian restaurant they went to on their first date.

Julie met Ken at the restaurant, and they got a table and had a drink before ordering their dinner. Julie thought he looked really nice in his blue shirt and khakis, all freshly shaven like he took a shower.

"Ken, you look so good at the end of the day. Did you go home and shower before meeting with me? You look wonderful. You don't need to go home and take a shower. You always smell good."

"I was working in the shop today, and they spilled some type of grease, and it got on me and my clothes, so I had to go home and shower."

"Now I am offended because I was excited that you got cleaned up for me."

He laughed. "I would like to invite you back to my place, and I will let you take a shower with me."

She laughed then saw that he was serious and said, "Oh well, I can do that."

They finished their dinner and had some dessert. They went to Ken's place, and they took a shower together. When Julie came out of the bathroom, Ken had candles lit and a glass of wine waiting for her. They made love for hours. It was stupendous and sexy. Their relationship was so much better now. Things had definitely moved on in their relationship, and they felt so comfortable with each other. They really knew each other now, and Ken really knew how to turn her on. He was very attentive to her sexually, and Julie liked it.

"It is getting late, Ken, and I better get home. We have to go to work tomorrow, you know. I had a really good time tonight."

"I enjoyed it more," Ken said.

"No," Julie said, "that would be impossible." Julie added, "I am looking forward to this cookout Saturday.

"Me too, I think it is going to be a great time." Ken said.

Julie left and drove home, thinking her life was getting awfully busy lately, but she was enjoying it very much. Julie got home really late, so Beth was in bed already. She headed right to bed. Mornings come too soon when you have been up this late. Julie looked at the clock, and it was 3:00 a.m. What a day and what a night!

Julie saw Beth in the morning, and she asked Julie if she came home really late last night.

"Oh no," Julie said, "I am caught!" They laughed.

"I am not checking up on you. I just went to bed late last night. I could not sleep thinking about school, and I was just all keyed up. I finally had a glass of wine and then fell asleep."

"Is there something bothering you about school, Beth?" asked Julie.

"No. I guess with work and school, I am feeling a little overwhelmed right now, but I will get used to it. I am sure."

"You have been out of school for a few years, and it is always hard to go back to studying, I have heard people say. I probably should go back for my masters too and need to think about that. I better get going. This is going to be a long day at work since I did not get much sleep. I will see you tonight."

Ken helped Julie get some things for the party on Saturday. They shopped most of the week every day after work. Julie really appreciated Ken helping. He bought a lot of the food. Beth and Julie shopped for the party appetizers and drinks. They also bought the firepit for out back and found some chairs in the basement to put around it. They felt if they got most of the place put together and set up, it would be just preparing food and drinks on Saturday.

Julie suggested, "We should have a housekeeper come in to clean for us, especially since my kids and their friends would be staying over."

"Julie, that is a great idea since I will have no energy to clean this whole house by Saturday," Beth said.

Beth arranged for the lady to come in and clean on Friday while they were at work. When they came home, the place looked really fresh and clean. She even cleaned the porches and the furniture out there, which was awesome. Beth did not even think about that. Beth and Julie went out to get their dinner, and Julie picked up some fresh flowers to put around.

"I am so excited about this party, and my friends are excited to come," Beth said.

"This is the first time we really did anything like this, and I just can't wait to see how it all turns out. I hope it goes well, and we can do it again some time," Julie said.

"Randy told me he will be bringing a three-layer dip and chips and some beer."

"That is nice. That is very northerner of him." They laughed. "They always make sure that the comfort food and the beer is on hand."

Beth and Julie really enjoyed getting ready for the party; it was exciting to have people over. They were running around like a couple of nuts, but it was fun. Beth said, "I did not realize how much work it takes to get this stuff together."

"It has been a while for me too, Beth, since I have planned a big cookout, and I am exhausted already," Julie said. "It is a lot of work."

Julie's kids came early and with a friend each. Harry brought his good buddy, Dave, and Stephanie brought her friend Hillary. They both were very nice, which should not surprise Julie. Stephanie had been dating a guy named Jack, but they had split up, which was unfortunate for Stephanie, but she had moved on since she was young. They all asked what they could do to help, which Julie felt was very thoughtful. Julie told them she would show them their rooms. Julie put out drinks and a snack for them when they came downstairs. They all helped finish getting things ready for the party and for the guests arriving.

CHAPTER 23

Ken, Sandy, and Mark arrived early around 5:30 p.m. They wanted to help with anything they needed them to do. Julie said, "Beth and I are putting out the appetizers and setting up the drinks. The guests should be showing up soon. Sandy, you look like you are definitely showing more this week."

"It has only been a week." Sandy laughed and said, "I guess it will be growing more each month." Julie thought she looked really pretty pregnant and happy. She and Mark were really good together and were making their marriage work. Ken went out and started the firepit. The guests started arriving, and Beth and Julie took turns answering the door and introducing everyone. Ken had asked some of the couples whom he and Julie had gone out with together. There were a total of thirty people.

Beth and Julie were really enjoying hosting. Beth said, "Why have we not done this before? I think we are pretty good at entertaining. Who knew?" They both laughed. Everyone interacted and talked and laughed and were really enjoying the evening. The weather turned out perfect, not too hot, just clear and pleasant. Some sat on the porches, and some sat around the firepit, but everyone seemed comfortable being here. Julie had never talked to so many people at one time that she really did not know that well. Stephanie and Harry seemed to be having a good time. Julie noticed Stephanie was a little quiet.

"Stephanie, is there something wrong?" Julie asked.

"Yes, Hillary has been hitting on Harry all night."

"Is there something wrong with that? I thought you liked her."

"Yes, but she is dating someone else, and I don't want her to hurt Harry. I really think Harry is interested in her and likes the attention."

"I don't think you should worry about Harry. He can take care of himself. Maybe he just likes the attention that she is giving him. Does he know that Hillary is seeing someone?"

"Yes, he does, so I am wondering what he is thinking."

"Do you know his friend Dave very well?"

"Yes."

"Maybe you should go over and talk to him for a while and then join Harry and Hillary."

"That is a good idea. Maybe I am overreacting."

When Stephanie joined Harry and Hillary, she could tell he was enjoying her company, and she saw them kiss. Stephanie just walked away and started talking to some other guests.

Julie noticed that one of the girls whom Beth invited was interested and a little too friendly with Ken. She was young and beautiful; whatever she was saying to him, he was interested. He was looking at her breasts that were hanging out as well as her long, skinny legs. How could Ken not be looking? Julie was a bit disappointed and hoped that no one else noticed, especially her kids. Seeing that would give them a bad idea about Ken. It did look like he was being polite with her, but he did not seem to walk away either. Julie thought he must like the attention. Julie was feeling exhausted and felt embarrassed. She went and poured herself a drink and pulled Beth aside.

"Who is your friend who is talking to Ken?"

"That is Nancy. I see that she has been clinging to Ken quite a bit tonight. I don't think you have anything to worry about, Julie. She is a nice girl and is just friendly to everyone, and you definitely don't have to worry about Ken. He is really into you."

"That is what I thought, but now I am feeling a little suspicious."

"Julie, don't go there. You are worrying about nothing."

Julie was looking at her, and she was jealous because she was much younger than her, and she thought maybe Ken was flattered by her. Julie told herself to stop and started mingling with the guests. Julie was talking with Sandy and Mark when Ken came over and put his arm around her.

"Are you enjoying the party?"

"Yes, I am really enjoying the party, and it looks like you are too."

"That sounds a little sarcastic to me, the way you said that. Is there something wrong?" Ken asked. Julie just looked at him as if looks could kill.

"No."

Ken asked, "Would you like something to eat or drink? I am going for a second helping."

"No, thanks," Julie said. "I just got myself a drink."

Ken walked away. A few minutes later, Julie looked over at Ken, and he was sitting at the table with Nancy again. This is a side of Ken that Julie had never seen before. She would not be able to forget it. He was no different from any other man, and that really hurt and disappointed her. She thought she better think more about their relationship and if she was ready for one after all as far as trusting. She might be better moving on. She would be better off alone rather than being with someone whom she couldn't look in the eye and see the real man that she thought she knew.

She never knew she had such trust issues. You think you know someone so well, and then it turns out that you don't know them at all, and it is a little scary. Relationships are a bit too complex, especially after wasting so much of her time with her ex-husband. That never made her happy. Why would she consider wasting her time again?

She tried to shake it off and went over to talk to some of the other guests. The rest of the night, she felt so angry that it was hard to keep up with the conversations around her. She thought, *Here I am giving advice to Stephanie, and I am acting just like she is. I need to take my own advice.*

"What is wrong with Julie, Beth?" Randy asked. "She is looking a little unhappy."

"I don't know," said Beth. "Maybe she is little tired. It has been a long day."

Beth was thinking she did not want tell him what was really going on. Beth admitted to herself that she would be concerned if she were Julie. Just watching those two together, she noticed they were being a bit flirty. *I think Nancy is putting the moves on Ken. I see that Ken is enjoying it. After what has happened between Larry and me, it seems that all men are the same. It just takes a flirt from a pretty girl, and they are in the game. Maybe later they will regret their actions just like Larry did. I am no fool, and I would never be able to look at him the same again. Over with a capital O. I am sure Randy noticed what Ken was doing, and everybody noticed. It was a little obvious. Ken does not know what he is getting himself into with Nancy. I feel bad for Julie,* Beth thought.

It was about 1:00 a.m. before everyone started to leave. Beth and Julie thanked them for coming; they all seemed to have a good time. "We could not have asked for a better evening," Beth said.

Sandy and Mark helped them clean up a little, and then Mark took her home. She was very tired; pregnancy will do that to you. Ken and Randy put out the fire and helped them clean up before saying good night. Julie's kids had called it a night earlier and went in to watch a special program they all liked on TV then headed to bed.

"This was really nice," Julie said. "We should do this again sometime this summer."

Beth said, "Randy and my friends got along well tonight. That was the first he had met them."

It was about 3:00 a.m. by the time they finished cleaning up and headed to bed. "Beth, I will be up early tomorrow and get breakfast started before the kids get up. They will be heading back to Wilmington after breakfast," Julie said.

The next morning, the kids got up, and Julie had breakfast and coffee waiting for them. They all seemed a little tired, but Julie thought not as tired as she was feeling. She was listening to them talking, and she thought that everything was okay between them because they all seemed like great friends again. Maybe it was just the evening being out at a party trying to enjoy the night.

Hillary and Dave thanked Beth and Julie for inviting them to the barbecue and letting them stay. Julie told them they were both welcome to come back anytime. Julie helped them pack up the car, and they were off to Wilmington. Julie went back into the house and told Beth that she was exhausted and needed another cup of coffee and a long hot shower. They went out on the porch to enjoy their coffee and the gorgeous morning.

Beth said, "It is so nice to have a day off and just hang out. I may go shopping today. Do you want to come, Julie?"

"No, I think I am just going to go do grocery shopping for the week ahead, and I need some things I have to pick up." The phone was ringing, and it was Ken calling, but she did not answer the phone.

Beth just looked at Julie. "What was that? Are you not talking to him?"

"I have to sort my feelings out. I am not clear what was going on with him and Nancy. I'm sorry. I know she is your friend, but how well do you know her?"

"She is very nice. I've never known her to be a flirt. Maybe she did not know that you and Ken date. I am not trying to defend her. You and I are great friends, and we are closer than I am with her, so I am on your side. I just never knew her to go after someone else's boyfriend, and it was a party. Maybe she was just out to have fun."

"She did know that Ken and I were a couple, I think. It was obvious when they came in, and we introduced everyone, and I specifically said my boyfriend, Ken. I don't know, Beth. It is not Nancy. It is Ken and the way he was acting around her. It is my gut feeling that he liked her and her attention, so I need to think about this before I speak to him."

"You do what you think you need to do. In the meantime, do you want me to talk to Nancy and see what she thought about the party? I will not let on about anything pertaining to Ken. I will just listen to see if she brings it up."

"Okay, that is a good idea. See if she was interested in him or if he was interested in her and let me know. I will call Ken back and see what he has to say."

Julie took a long hot shower and got dressed to go to the store. She returned Ken's call while she got dressed. "Hi, I am sorry I missed your call. How are you?"

"I wanted to take you out to lunch or dinner today. Whichever you prefer?" Ken asked.

"Oh, I am a little exhausted today. I am going to go shopping and come back and relax today."

Ken said, "Oh, okay. Then I guess I will just hang out here at my apartment and do laundry. I really enjoyed the party yesterday. It was really nice."

"I am glad you had a good time. It seemed everyone did. I did not get to bed until three, so I am really tired today."

"I am sorry to hear that, but if you change your mind, give me a call."

"Okay," she said and hung up.

She just couldn't get over how he acted with her, and she was feeling he was being little two-faced. Maybe she should have gone with him to lunch just to see what he would say or talk about. She went down and told Beth that she talked to him and declined his invitation to lunch or dinner today.

"Do you think I should call him back and go to see how he acts or what he has to say, if anything, about last night?"

"No, take the day, Julie, and think about it some more. Let me talk to Nancy and see what she has to say."

"Okay, then I am out the door to the store. I am looking forward to just watching TV and hanging out. I just may eat some leftovers from last night when I get back. You can join me. Maybe we can find a good movie to watch."

"That sounds good," said Beth. "See you later."

Sandy called to say that she and Mark had a good time at the barbecue. She said, "I just got up. Mark went to Starbucks to get one of his fancy coffees, so I thought I would give you a call. Julie, who was that girl that was with Ken all night?"

"That was Beth's friend, Nancy."

"Oh, why did you let her hang with him?" Sandy asked.

"Sandy, did you get that impression that he was hanging out with her too?" asked Julie.

Sandy hesitated but said, "Yes."

"I am really furious with him, Sandy. I don't know what to think or say, but I did not like his actions, and now I am concerned about him. I got the impression that he liked the attention, and if it is anything more than that, I don't know. He called me to go to lunch or dinner today, but I told him I had some things to do. I just don't want to talk to him until I sort it out in my head."

"That's a good idea," said Sandy, "because I got the impression that he enjoyed her company also. I just did not want to say it before you did. Don't jump to conclusions, though. Julie, he has been really nice to you all this time. Maybe he was just having an insecure night and needed some attention."

"Well," Julie said, "if that is the case, then I guess I am not good enough to make him feel good about himself."

Mark walked in the door with his fancy coffee and handed Sandy a bear claw from Starbucks.

"Thanks. Are you trying to make me look a little bigger, Mark?"

"No, you look beautiful, and you're pregnant, so you can look a little bigger is a healthy look for you."

"Well then, I am going to enjoy it." He gave her a big kiss. "I just got off the phone with Julie. She is trying to figure out what went on with Ken last night. What do you think was going on?"

"I think he was just being friendly, that's all. What did you think was going on, Sandy? I really think that you both are making this out to be more than what it is. It was a barbecue, a get-together, and everyone was enjoying themselves, including you and me mingling with the crowd."

"Spoken like a man," said Sandy. "You all act like it is nothing, but it seems to a woman, when you are involved with someone, that the attention should go to the one that you are in the relationship with, not with someone you have just met."

"No, I don't think he was thinking about that. I think he was just being social."

Sandy thought, *Just social! I think flirting men just do it without thinking about women's feelings. I know I was single once not so long ago. I am so impressed with Mark now, and I think I am really in love with him. He really shows a lot of love and care for me. It is outstanding, and I was not impressed with his lovemaking in the beginning, but it has definitely improved since then. I am really happy. I can't wait to see how he is as a father. I have watched him with his brother's kids when we were visiting, and he really likes kids. I really like this condo too. It is so nice, and we are getting the nursery put together, so it will be perfect for the baby. Mark brings something home every time he goes to the store for the baby. We will be finding out the sex of the baby next week when we go for the ultrasound, and Mark wants to be there with me.*

CHAPTER 24

Julie thought she would call Ken and tell him that she was thinking about getting together for dinner but then thought she wanted to hear what Nancy said to Beth. Then she would know a little more how to deal with Ken. She knew what she needed to do about it, just wanted to hear the truth that she already knew in her heart.

She got home and put the groceries away and started on her laundry for the week. She just couldn't stop thinking about what to do or how to handle it. She did not want to look like a fool to him or let him think that he could get away with this behavior when he was supposed to be in a relationship with her. Everything was going so well with them; he was so supportive, and they enjoyed each other's company so well. They just seemed to fit well together; she just didn't understand.

What would her kids say? They already met him and were so impressed with him. They were going to start to think there was something wrong with their mother. Julie decided to have a glass of wine. Why not just relax? It was her day off after all. She was sitting in the den, looking at her emails, when Beth came home.

"How was your shopping trip?" Julie called to her from the den.

"I found a lot of sales and bought myself the prettiest dresses and pants."

"Great, come join me with a glass of wine. It is my day off, and I am relaxing."

Bringing her glass of wine with her, Beth said, "I talked to Nancy today."

"What did she say?"

"You are not going to like it. Nancy felt that he was coming on to her and that she really enjoyed his company. Ken said to her at the end of the party, 'Hopefully I will see you again.'"

"Ken said that? So he let her believe that he was indeed interested in her."

"Yes, that is the impression Nancy got. I did not mention you, and neither did she."

"Wow, that hurts. I don't know what to say. Tell me what to say, Beth. I am dumbfounded and feel like an idiot. When you think you know someone so well—and I know we all keep saying that statement over and over again, but it's true—it really does hurt. I am not telling you anything you don't already know, am I?"

"No, I have been there already. That is for sure. I really know how you are feeling," said Beth. "All I can say is, like you told me, it is good you found out now rather than later."

"Well said," said Julie. "You are right. Now I need to talk to him and see what he has to say for himself, only out of curiosity, and so the next relationship, I will be wiser."

Julie was feeling very depressed and letdown. She just couldn't stop thinking about Ken long enough to go to sleep. Julie didn't feel she would be able to see Ken again. He could just move on because she needed to have respect for herself. He had turned out to be an asshole. She started to read a book to relax herself and take her mind off everything before falling to sleep. She felt like she was going through a divorce again.

After work on Monday, Ken called Julie to see if they could get together that evening. Julie took a deep breath, thinking of what to do. *Maybe I will see him and tell him that it is over between us and the reason. I think that I should get that off my chest and move on.* She could not get it off her mind all day at work.

Julie called Ken back. "Yes, Ken, you come over."

"Okay, I will be there after dinner."

Julie made some iced tea and baked a batch of cookies. She thought cookies would be nice to have around, and she needed something to keep herself occupied. Then she thought she would make a pasta salad for herself and Beth for later. That would be a surprise for Beth because she was the one who likes to cook, not her.

Beth came walking into the kitchen and said, "What are you doing? Are you feeling ambitious or something?"

"I am trying to keep myself busy, Beth. Ken is coming over, and I am nervous about what I am going to say. I have decided to go with my feelings and just tell him it is over and why. I am not going to spare words or feelings."

Beth looked at Julie, knowing exactly how she was feeling, and did not know what to say. "I feel a little bad that I invited Nancy, and she seems to be the culprit to all of this."

"No, it was not your friend Nancy that did this. It was Ken. Nancy set the bait, and he went for it, so it is Ken's fault. He was the one who was drooling all over her," Julie stated.

Ken arrived at 7:00 p.m. He came in and gently kissed Julie hello. Julie kissed him back because she thought that would be the last time she would feel his closeness again. She offered him some iced tea and said, "Let's go out on the porch and talk."

He gave her an incredulous look.

Julie said, "We need to talk, Ken, about the night of the barbecue. I noticed that you seemed occupied with that girl Nancy and really seemed to enjoy her company."

"Julie, that is not true. I was just being friendly to her, nothing else," Ken said.

"I am not stupid, Ken. You were with her all night and right in front of me. I don't think you spoke to me most of the night because you were entertaining her. Other people also noticed that you were enticed with her and she was hanging all over you. Ken, I don't want to see you again. I will never feel that I could trust you ever. If you could do that right in front of me, then I don't know what you would be doing when I am not with you."

"Julie, I am not interested in anyone but you. If I gave you and others that impression, I am sorry. That is not me. I am not like that. I would not do anything to hurt you. I feel you and I have something special together, and I don't want you to tell me that it is over. You are making a mistake, Julie," Ken said.

"No, it is over. I did not realize that maybe I am not ready for a relationship right now, and maybe that is true for you also. Ken, you did seem interested in the attention that that girl gave you. She was all over you. Nancy told Beth that you told her that you wanted to see her again. That is all I needed to know, so there you are, free to pursue her. I'm done with you," Julie said.

Ken looked really hurt, but she told him to just leave. She did not want to hear any more excuses or sappy stories. He was caught, pure and simple. He got up and left. Julie felt relieved but devastated. She went up to bed, curled up in a ball, and cried for quite a while. She got up and looked at herself in the mirror and suddenly felt and looked old. *Thank you, Ken, for making me feel so good about myself,* she thought. She was proud of herself that she was able to stand her ground with him and did not listen to his lies. Later, after she'd settled down, she went downstairs to talk to Beth.

"Ken and I talked, and I asked him to leave."

Beth said, "I hope this was a misunderstanding and you don't regret this because I do think that he has strong feelings for you."

Julie said, "You know, Beth, you could be right, but do I want to be with someone who can deceive me right in front of my face and act like he did nothing wrong? I always say if it is meant to be, it will be. But apparently, not with him. I think I will join the gym and work out. That will give me something to do so I can stay in shape and maybe someday feel good about myself again. That will give me time to sort through my feelings and get on with my life. I really need to move into the direction of me."

Beth laughed. "Julie, you are funny."

Julie said, "I am beginning to realize that I am stronger than I thought I was. I am also going to call a realtor and start looking at homes to buy. The kids will be able to move in with me if they want when they graduate from college. You can also move in, Beth. You are like one of my kids but more of a friend—and a mature confidante."

"Julie, I don't know what to say. I am honored. Thank you," Beth said.

"I am so glad that I have you and Sandy to talk to. My friend Diane will be coming this Thursday. I think I mentioned that to you. I am looking forward to time off from work and her visit. I am a little embarrassed that I have to tell her the man of my dreams turned into a frog overnight." They both laughed.

Beth asked, "Julie, you did say she is divorced, right? I am sure she knows what men are like."

"I know, Beth. She is my old friend, and it will be nice to talk to her and catch up."

When Ken left Julie's, his face was red and burning, and he felt devastated and numb. He thought that he and Julie were okay together; they were a team and in love. He had such strong feelings for her, and he did not want to lose her, but he guessed he did. He did like the attention that Nancy was giving him, and he did say that maybe they would see each other again, but he did not seriously mean it. What was he thinking? Stupid. She was younger than what he would be attracted to, a little immature for him, but again, he was flattered.

Maybe Julie was right. They were moving too fast since they both had gone through divorces. He would have asked her out, and really, he did think about it, but he had strong feelings for Julie. Julie made him feel like a real man and flattered him the way she looked at him. He would get her back, he hoped, and sometime soon. He would give her some time to calm down and try to talk to her again.

Beth decided to go meet up with some of her friends for shopping and dinner the next day, but she was really concerned about Julie. She was going to ask her to go out with them but thought she probably needed sometime alone right now. Besides, Nancy might be there, and that would not be a good thing. They had all been through so much; life can be very confusing.

Beth's schooling was going well, thank goodness, and she had been covering a lot of classes. She should have her master's degree in about a year. Having the classes online had really given her the time and opportunity to pursue her degree and continue to work. She still didn't know where to go from there when their lease was up. She should continue to look at places to rent that were close to work. The only thing was, when she got her degree, she would be making more money, and then maybe she could buy a home, or maybe a condo near the city would be nice. She liked the neighborhood, so it would be easy to stay there where she was familiar.

This weekend Beth would be going out with Randy; maybe she could talk him into looking at some properties with her just to see what she could afford and where. She really liked the thought of living with Julie; it was so nice of her to think of her like that. At least she had that option.

CHAPTER 25

The week went fast, and Julie was so happy to see her old friend.

"Please come in, Diane. It has been such a long time since we have seen each other, and you look wonderful," Julie said. "I must look like hell, but I will tell you about it after you get settled. I'll help you with your bags and show you the room you will be staying in. I want you to make yourself comfortable, and then we can talk. I will have lunch and some iced tea ready for you when you come down."

"Okay, thanks, Julie. I am starving."

Diane came down, looking a little tired from her trip. "This house is beautiful. You were lucky to find this to rent. Your landlord leases this house, right? Maybe he will want to sell it, and you can buy it, Julie."

"No, I think this would be out of my price bracket, Diane."

"Well, it would be worth looking into it just to see what the market is and what he would ask for it."

"You're right. I will look into it. I do love everything about it: the layout and all the rooms. It would be perfect if Harry and Stephanie want to move back in with me. I was just thinking about getting into the house market because my lease will be up in several months, and I definitely need to know where I will be going. There has just been so much happening lately that I feel a little overwhelmed with everything."

"Like what?"

"Well, you know about Mary dying, and Sandy and Mark were married, and she moved in with him since they are expecting a baby soon. Remember I told you about Ken and I dating? Well, I broke up with him just this week. I could not wait for you to meet him, and then something happened. I am still recovering from it. I thought he was so special. He has met my kids, and they really liked him. Last weekend we had a barbecue and had invited friends from work. Ken stayed attached to this woman, Nancy, that Beth invited and flirted with her right in front of my eyes. Woman—I should say 'girl.' She is only in her early twenties, which is a real blow to my ego. I should not have gotten into a relationship. It was too soon for both of us. He called me, and then he came over.

"We talked about it, or I talked about it with him, of how letdown I was with him. Told him that I just can't be with him when he enjoyed himself with that girl all night right in front of my eyes. Even my friends said they saw him flirting with that girl, and they were shocked too. I did not want to hear what he had to say. I told him it was over and asked him to just leave. I don't want to second-guess someone all the time. I am done with him. It was so embarrassing and humiliating in front of our guests and my friends, Diane. It was awful. Now just saying that makes me feel better because

I will not go through the rest of my life with doubts about the man I want to spend the rest of my life with."

"I agree," said Diane, "and it may have been too soon for both of you to get involved since it has only been a little more than a year since your divorce. I, too, was involved with someone, and it did not work out, and I have been divorced a couple of years. I don't know if I am looking for Mr. Too Perfect or if I just feel that I am happy alone."

"I am so glad you're here. I really needed an old friend, and I missed you," Julie said. "We have so much catching up to do, and I know this weekend is going to go by fast. Tomorrow I want to show you around Raleigh. Beth will be coming home from work soon, and she can join us. If you don't mind, I will call Mark and Sandy to see if they can come over later."

"I would like that."

"I want to grill some steaks and have a cookout tonight. I really want you to meet everyone."

"I am looking forward to meeting them too," Diane said.

Diane and Julie talked for hours, catching up on their lives, and after Diane went up to shower and freshen up for the evening, Julie called Sandy to invite her and Mark over to meet Diane and enjoy a cookout with just the five of them and have some drinks.

Beth arrived home after work, and Julie introduced her to Diane, and they all started to put their dinner together. They marinated the steaks and made the salad and side dishes. Julie had even baked a cake earlier. It was simple, not like last weekend, when there were a lot of people to serve. The evening was nice and ended too soon; they enjoyed the company. Julie was really happy to introduce Diane to every one of her new friends. She told all of them about breaking up with Ken.

Sandy said, "I am not surprised after what we all witnessed that night."

Julie felt a little hurt by that statement, but it was true and, again, embarrassing.

"I am going to show Diane around town tomorrow and see if I can talk her into moving here with us."

"Yes, right," said Diane. "It is nice, but then again, I would like to find a job like the rest of you did before I could make the move. It is really nice here. This weather is great, a little hot, but I could get used to it."

The weekend did go too fast, and Diane and Julie said their goodbyes. Diane promised that she would come back soon, maybe in the winter, when it was warm and Connecticut was cold. Julie decided to clean up and call the kids and tell them about the weekend. Stephanie was seeing someone, and Julie wanted to see how that was going, and she needed to meet this person. She better tell them that she and Ken were no longer seeing each other without going into details. She and Harry didn't need to know all the dirt, but then she wondered if they noticed Ken with that girl. They would probably tell her if they noticed.

This week she would call a loan officer to see what she could afford and then talk to the landlord to see if he had thought of selling the house. Like Diane said, it was worth looking into. She still would like to see some other homes.

CHAPTER 26

Julie talked to some of the girls at work about the housing market in Raleigh. One of the girls, Martha, had just bought a house and invited her over to see it after work. When Julie arrived at the house, she could see that the neighborhood was really nice and her house was just beautiful. Julie toured Martha's house and then had a drink of wine. Martha told her that the realtor, Thomas Smart, who worked with her did a really good job, and she would be happy to refer him to her.

"That would be nice," said Julie, "but I need to see my loan officer first to see what I can afford, and then I will contact him."

Driving home, Julie thought she should talk to the landlord first to see if he was interested in selling the house. She would definitely prefer the house she was living in; it had all the accommodations that she needed.

Beth got home from work and thought how quiet the house was. There was a letter from the court system that they wanted Sandy, Julie, and her to testify in court on Mary's behalf and put the guy away for good. Beth still couldn't believe all that had happened, and she just couldn't stop thinking about Mary. That was so sad, and now she was gone because of some creep whom she loved. *I will definitely be there in court. Life is tough!* she thought.

When Julie came in, Beth showed her the letter. They both cried and hugged each other. "It is too sad, but I will be there. You bet I will. And I hope he rots in jail for life. Mary would still be here if it weren't for him."

"I actually hope they give him the death sentence."

Beth and Julie sat and had a glass of wine, something to soothe them a little bit. "I am looking into buying a house, Beth. I was thinking of asking the landlord if he is interested in selling this house. I have to get qualified first, so tomorrow after work, I am going to go meet with a loan officer to see what I can afford."

"Wow, that would be great for you. Then you will have a house, and when your kids get out of school, they will have somewhere to go. I don't know what I am going to do, Julie. I am not sure if I am ready to buy a house right now."

"You're young, Beth. You have plenty of time to figure out your future. My time is running out. I would like to offer for you to live with me if I get a house until you figure things out. Would you want to do that?"

"Really? You would want me to move in with you?"

"Yes, I am getting used to having you around. I would be lost without you."

"Then it's a deal. I would love to do that, so hurry up and buy."

They both laughed. They heard the door open, and Sandy walked in crying. She had gotten the letter from the courts.

"I am going to testify. I will be as big as a bear by then, but I will be there to testify against this animal."

"I don't think we knew all the story, but we do know enough that she was intimidated by him and wanted to be left alone," Julie said.

The next day after work, Julie met with her loan officer at the bank. She filled out all the forms he needed to determine her qualifications. He told her he would do a credit check and have the qualification amount as soon as tonight. Julie thanked him and left. On the way home, Julie was thinking how nice it would be to get settled into her new home. It would feel like she had roots again. She really loved it in Raleigh with all her new friends and job. This was going to be great. She just knew it.

Later that night, the loan officer called and told Julie what she qualified for, and she was so excited about it. She could not believe she could afford so much. The loan officer told her she would have to have 20 percent down and have 10 percent for closing costs. He told her that if she had more money to put down, it would lower her monthly mortgage payment. Julie thought, *It really paid off. I have been putting money away plus what I have in savings from my ex and splitting the sale of our house.* "Wow, I can't wait to get started on this." She yelled to Beth that she was qualified to buy a house, and they jumped for joy. "Let's go out to eat and celebrate."

CHAPTER 27

Sandy looked at Mark. "Are you going to love me when I get as big as a house?"

"I am going to keep loving you. You just get more and more beautiful carrying our child," Mark said. "Let's go shopping and get this little guy some clothes since we know it's a boy. Then we should shop for you and get you some pretty maternity dresses. I want to keep you looking your best and feeling great about yourself."

"That is so sweet, Mark. That sounds like fun. Let's go now and stop and get something to eat while we are out. They are probably having good sales this weekend, and I want to get as much as we can...Ouch!"

"What is the matter, Sandy?"

"I don't know. I just had a really sharp pain in my stomach."

"You better sit down awhile. We can always go shopping tomorrow."

Sandy bent over with the pain. "I think we better call the doctor. Something is going on."

Mark called the doctor, and they told them to go right to the emergency room, and he would meet them there.

When they got there, Sandy started to bleed, and they were really scared. They told the nurse that the doctor was going to meet them there, and they checked her in and put her in a bed. While they were getting Sandy settled, Mark went out to call Julie and Beth so they could come and give him some support if things started to go bad. They told Mark that they would be right over. When Beth and Julie arrived at the hospital, they saw Mark, who looked really distraught.

"What is happening?" asked Julie.

"I don't know," Mark said. "The doctor just got here. He is examining her now. She started having sharp pains and then bleeding when we got here. We were on our way out to go shopping for the baby, and she doubled over with pain. I hope nothing happens to either of them. I don't know what I would do."

"Well, I am sure they will be all right. It just may be false labor. It happens to pregnant women all the time, but it is a good thing you got her here. It's not a good idea to put things like this off and not get checked."

Just then, the doctor came out. "Mark, it could be false labor or she has pre-eclampsia. We are going to keep her overnight and run more tests so that we can see for sure to be on the safe side. I'm sure everything is going to be all right," the doctor said.

After they put Sandy in her room, they all went in to see her. She looked a little pale but good. "Are you trying to give us a scare, Sandy?" Julie said.

"I am starting to feel a little better. The pain came on so fast, and the doctor gave me something for pain and nausea. I don't know what I would do if anything would happen to this baby."

"Do you want Beth or me to call your parents and let them know what is going on?"

"No, we better wait until tomorrow. I am glad I have all of you here for me. That makes me feel better," Sandy said.

Beth said, "Julie and I better get going so you can get some rest, but we will be here if you need us. Just call."

Julie said, "We will see you tomorrow at home. I'm sure everything is all right."

On Sunday morning, Julie called her landlord. "Hi, George. It is Julie. Do you have a minute to talk to me?"

"Yes, sure, Julie. Is everything all right?"

"Oh, yes, I wanted to ask you something I have been thinking about. I am looking for a house to buy, and I was wondering if you would consider selling this house to me. Of course, I do not know if you were even thinking about selling, but I thought I would ask anyway. I don't know what you would ask for it, but if you are willing to sell, we could talk about it."

"Well Julie, I've never given it a thought about selling the house. I would have to think about it and talk to my wife. I may have a hard time letting go of it since I grew up in that house. I don't know. Let me think about this, and I will get back to you," George said.

"Thank you. I did not mean to upset you. I just thought if you were thinking about it. Just think about it, George, and call me."

Mark called later that day and said that Sandy was just fine and he was taking her home. The doctor said it was false labor and that a lot of women go through that at this stage of pregnancy.

"We were both really relieved," Mark said. "This is all new to both of us."

"Well, that is good news," Julie said. "Is it okay if Beth and I come over? We will bring dinner with us. There is that little steak chophouse. We can stop and get takeout. Does that sound good to you, Mark?"

"That would be fine. We will see you at dinnertime then."

Beth and Julie stopped at the chophouse to pick up the order then headed over to see Sandy and Mark.

"Sandy, you look wonderful. I am glad everything is okay," Julie said.

"You had us worried," said Beth.

Mark asked Julie if she had heard anything more from Ken.

"No, and I don't think I will."

"I ran into him the other day," Mark said. "He said he was not flirting with that girl, and you overreacted. It was just all innocent. He said he was going to call you and try to talk to you some more about it."

"I have nothing more to say, and I don't feel that I over-reacted. That tells me that he has no respect for me and my feelings. I thought we had more between us. I did really like him, and I just feel disappointed and letdown, and I don't think that will ever go away."

"I just wanted you to know that I talked to him. It is up to you to decide if you want to talk to him or not."

Sandy asked, "Beth, are you still dating Randy?"

"I am, but I am playing the field, as they say. I don't want to get involved while I am going to school. I want to get my degree and improve on my career for now."

"You will do well, Beth. I know it. I am thinking after the baby is born, maybe taking classes to improve my skills. Maybe I will be able to study while he sleeps, but I know I will be busy and be without sleep for a while."

"You got that right," Julie said. "I think it is time for us to go, Beth, and let Sandy get some rest."

CHAPTER 28

Julie got a call from the realtor, Thomas Smart, whom her friend had mentioned. He wanted to know if she would be interested in looking at some houses after work on Tuesday.

"Yes, I would like to look at just a few so that I can get an idea of what I like and what is available. I can meet you at your office Tuesday at 5:30 p.m."

"Great," Thomas said. "I will see you and look forward to meeting you."

On Tuesday after work, Julie drove over to the realtor's office. The receptionist showed her to a conference room and told her that she would let the realtor know that she was there. Julie's jaw dropped when he walked in; he was drop-dead gorgeous, tall, had black hair, and had dimples when he smiled. He shook her hand and said, "I am Thomas, Julie. It is nice to finally meet you. I have set up a few houses to take a look at, and if you want to see more, we can always meet another evening or this coming weekend."

Thomas kept looking at Julie, thinking how adorable she was with her brown hair, big brown eyes, and a smile that just warmed you through. They started off with a house that was not far from where she was living. It was an older home, also brick, and on a small lot. "This is a nice lot, not too big."

When they walked into the house, it had mahogany stairs and trim and hardwood floors throughout. *I like the style of this house. It's not too big but has lots of room,* Julie thought. After they toured the house, Thomas asked what she thought of it.

"I like it. I am really hoping that the landlord will sell me his house where I am living now, but I doubt that will happen. I would like to see more if you don't mind, but this may be a contender."

"Sure, I have two more set up for you to look at this evening."

Julie kept thinking about how handsome he was and wondered what it would be like to date him; he was so courteous and polite. *When will I learn? I am ridiculous. I need some time before I start dating again! I really don't have a good sense of men at this stage in my life. I don't even know if he is married. I will look at his ring finger.* The next two houses were, again, very nice.

"I think you know exactly what I need. The kitchen in that last one was really spacious and big. Thank you so much for spending this time with me this evening, Thomas. I will call you soon to see more if that is okay with you."

"Yes, call anytime. If it is okay with you, I will give you a call and see what you have decided and if you want to look at more houses."

Julie's phone rang. It was her landlord, George. "Hi, George."

"I have still not decided yet, Julie, but I do want to have an appraiser come out to the house on Wednesday and give me an idea of the price value. Would it be okay with you if he comes with me Wednesday during the day?"

"That would be fine, George."

"Thank you. I will talk to you again soon."

Wow, thought Julie, *this is a good sign. He is definitely thinking about it, so that is good news for me.* Feeling anxious all week, Julie could not wait to see if the landlord wanted to sell or not. The realtor kept calling to set up other homes for her to see, but she was really stuck on this one. She had gotten used to the house, and she liked everything about it and wanted it. She wanted to be settled once and for all with a nice home for Stephanie and Harry to come home to and know that it was home and that she would not be moving again. She got through the days at work, and she still had been peeking at other homes. There were nice homes out there; in fact, there was one she looked at similar to this one, so if this did not come through, she would buy that one.

Julie saw Beth when she got home from work and told her, "I am going crazy waiting to hear about this house, Beth. However, I have another one that I like, and it is very similar to this one. Beth, you are going to move in with me, aren't you?"

"Yes, and I can't wait. I need to know if I have to pack my stuff or keep it as it is. I would like to know too because school is consuming me, and with work, I have a heavy plate right now."

"I will let you know as soon as I know, Beth. Honestly I think we both need to go out and get something to drink. Do you agree?"

"Yes," said Beth, "let's do it. I don't have school tonight or any studies to do, so let's go."

"Beth, you should see the realtor, Thomas. He is gorgeous. I am going to call him to see more houses with him this weekend. I enjoy his company and his knowledge about the housing market."

"Sure you do, Julie." Beth laughed. "Good for you. You're moving on too."

"We sure have learned a lot in this past year. Haven't we?"

As they entered the restaurant, Julie saw Ken sitting at a table with another woman. Her heart skipped a beat.

Beth said, "Should we just leave or stay?"

"I want to stay," said Julie. "I will be running into him from time to time anyway. Raleigh is not a big city. I may as well get used to it."

"The woman does seem very attractive. It is not Nancy, and he did not notice us yet."

"I feel jealous for sure," said Julie. "I really did want it to work for us, but unfortunately, it would never feel right again between us. It looks like he has moved on quickly. When you trust someone and have given yourself so completely and then been deceived by them, you can never look at him the same way again. You don't believe a word he says to you. Even if it is a compliment, it always will feel like an empty compliment. When my ex and I were married, he never talked, so I thought he always had something on his mind that he did not want to share with me, but after the years went by, I realized that is who he is. He is just not a sharing person in any way. I am so glad we finally made the split. I would rather be alone than be with him. I do know that for sure. Okay, I am going on. I will stop now."

Beth said, "Let's order a drink, and if you need to talk about it, Julie, talk. I will listen."

"I just want to move forward at this stage in my life and get settled to know where I will be now, not in the future. I am not going to let a man choose my life or my future. I feel that I now have control of my own destiny. You're young, Beth. Don't let anything I say change your ways. You're smart and will learn to handle your life as it happens. All situations are different, and not all men are jerks. I want to believe that. I am sure you will find one that is right for you."

"I hope so," Beth said, "but right now I am content."

Ken looked over and saw Julie sitting with Beth at the table across the room. Unsure how to react, he just looked and then focused on his date. If she acknowledged him, he would just say hello. They had just ordered, so it would be awkward to tell her date that they should leave without an excuse. He sat there and kept conversing with his date, who was really a nice girl, and he did enjoy her company. However, he did want things to work out for him and Julie. Maybe in time she would come around to him again. If she would let him talk to her at some point, it might work. He looked over again, and Julie saw him looking. They both nodded acknowledgment of each other, but no one made a move toward the other.

"Beth, Ken just noticed us sitting here. He looked over. I don't know what I should do."

"Just sit here. He is with a date, Julie. Just don't do anything and drink your drink. Let's order an appetizer. I am getting hungry. It is our night out to relax, remember?"

"Yes, you're right. Let's drink and be merry, as they say."

"This reminds me about the time we ran into Larry. It was devastating."

"I know! I was not there that night. That must have been awful since you did not know about the other woman. I have been apart from Ken for a while now, so this is a little different and not as hurtful as what you went through."

Beth said, "That girl looks familiar, though. I have seen her somewhere before."

"Where, Beth?"

"I don't know. It will come to me. I don't know her. I just have seen her before."

"Could it be someone at work?"

"I think it was at the company Christmas party. Maybe she was dating someone from work because I have never seen her at work."

"That is possible. If she is single, she would be dating different people. Maybe we should just order an appetizer to go?" said Julie.

"That is not fair, Julie. We can't keep running away from this kind of thing. We have to face up to it and go on with our dinner."

"Yes, we can do this. Let's change the subject."

"Well, look at it this way. Let him look over with regrets and weep. Does that make you feel better?"

"Yes, I think it does. Thanks, Beth, you are a very wise girl!"

CHAPTER 29

Julie returned from work. Beth was smiling and excited. "We are going to the hospital! Sandy has gone into real labor this time, and the baby is on the way."

"Oh, isn't this too early for her to deliver? I hope things go well! Let's go," said Julie.

"She may have it before we get there," Beth said. "When Mark called, he said her water broke, and they had just arrived at the hospital. They were waiting on the doctor to check her."

"Great! I can't wait to see this baby! Did they say what they were going to name him?"

"I am not sure they picked a name yet," said Beth.

When they arrived at the hospital, Mark came out to meet them. He said the doctor was in there with her now and that she was in a lot of pain. Two nurses went rushing by them into the room. One nurse came over and told Mark to go in, now that Sandy was ready to deliver, if he wanted to be there when the baby was born. He rushed right in, and Beth and Julie just looked at each other and smiled.

It was about an hour later when Mark came out smiling and announced proudly that it was a boy, and his name was

Marcus Luke. They gave him a big hug and congratulated him. He told them Sandy would be in recovery for a while and that they were taking the baby to the nursery to get cleaned up. They told him that they would go home and come back later to see them both. He was going to call their families and give them the news.

"Sandy's mother will be coming to help when we get home with the baby, so she really needs a heads-up so she can book her flight here. Sandy will only be in the hospital for two days."

"We will help any way we can," said Julie, "until she gets here."

"Julie and I are going shopping to get some diapers and other things for her and the baby and meet you back here." Beth said, "Let's go by the mall and pick something up for this little boy. They said they needed to buy clothes for him. It will be fun."

They left the hospital and went to the mall and found some really neat little outfits for the baby and a little going-home outfit. They also picked up diapers and more bottles and formula.

"Julie, are you going to help her until her mother gets here, or should we just leave her on her own?"

"If they want me to, I can help them get set up, make formula, and have bottles ready for them when she comes home. I am sure they will let us know if they need us."

After stopping and getting something to eat, they picked up some flowers and headed back to the hospital with the gifts.

Sandy was sitting there, looking really good and glowing like a new mother should.

"Hey, come over and see our little boy. He is sleeping here in his bassinet." Julie and Beth both smiled and walked over to the bassinet. "He has black hair, and his name is Marcus Luke." Beth and Julie doted over the baby with the proud parents.

"We brought you some flowers and some things for Marcus."

"Thank you," said Sandy. "That is wonderful."

"If you want me to help you until your mother gets here, just let me know," Julie said, "and I will take off of work a couple days."

"That is really nice of you, Julie. My mother should be here when I am released from the hospital, but thank you."

Mark just could not stop smiling like such a proud father. "I am so glad her mother is coming because I don't have a clue what to do with a baby. I have never been around too many kids."

"Oh," said Julie, "you will learn really fast, believe me."

"My parents are coming after Sandy's mother leaves and staying for the week. We are going to be doing a lot of entertaining, which is nice, and I do want you two to come over and meet everyone, so keep some time open for us."

"That sounds nice," said Beth. "I can't wait to meet your parents."

The next day, Julie got a call from Thomas. Julie thought, *I don't want to look at any houses. I just want to hear from the landlord telling me he is selling the house to me.*

"Hi, Julie. I wanted to know if you would be interested in going to a movie this weekend."

Feeling a little surprised to be asked on a date by Thomas, Julie said, "Yes, I haven't seen a movie in a long time." *The last time was with Ken,* she thought.

"I will pick you up on Saturday at seven. See you then."

Julie's phone rang again, and it was Ken. "I would like to see you and talk to you. Julie, please don't put me off."

"I thought you found someone, Ken. You looked like you were having a good time the other night."

"It was just a date, Julie, and that was a little awkward."

"It was awkward for me too, but I guess we will be seeing each other from time to time. This is not a real big city, so it is inevitable, and we will have to get used to that."

"I really need to see you. I want to talk with you. This is a big misunderstanding, and I really need to talk. I miss you."

Julie sighed. "I am busy this week, Ken. Sandy and Mark had their baby, and I will be helping them out, and I have a date this weekend."

"Well, maybe sometime in the future, I will give you a call, and I hope you will see me. It would mean a lot to me. I will call again. Goodbye."

Julie was feeling really sad after hanging up. *I really did love him. At least I thought I did, but I just can't do it again. I think I better just move on. I don't really know if he is sincere or not. I will never know that.*

Beth woke up on Saturday morning excited to go see Sandy and the baby since they came home. Sandy's mother should be there, so she would take over some bagels and donuts. Getting up and moving to the shower, she looked at the clock and could not get over how late it was: ten o'clock already. She quickly showered and dressed and went to the store. She was planning this evening to go out with some friends. She heard Julie saying that she was going out with Thomas tonight. She was happy for her.

She had not heard from Randy this week; he must be out of town. It had been nice dating him. They didn't see each other too often, which was good. She didn't want to get serious with him. She needed to get her master's degree and pursue her career right now, but she wanted to continue seeing him. It was time for her now and others later. She hoped Julie got this house, and then she could stay and pay her rent without moving. Otherwise, she had no idea where she would go, and their lease was up in September. She thought maybe she would go and look at some apartments again tomorrow.

CHAPTER 30

On Sunday morning, Julie told Beth about how her date went the night before.

"He is really a handsome man, and he is a talker. I can see why he is a realtor. He is going to pull me some comps for this neighborhood so I will get an idea of what the cost should be. I do have an idea of the cost, but it will be nice to see it on paper. I hope I am not getting my hopes up about this, Beth, and then get letdown. George did have an appraiser come through this week, so I thought just maybe that he would call. I did tell you that Ken called last week. He wants to see me, but I told him I had a date this weekend, and he said he will call to talk again soon. He told me he misses me, and I am really confused. I can't keep thinking about it."

"Maybe you should see him," Beth said, "and hear again what he has to say. He must really like you, even after we saw him with the date. He must be trying to move on without you but can't. Go see him when you are ready."

"Beth, you of all people are telling me to see him. I am shocked! I will eventually. Maybe, huh! I am going over to see Sandy and Mark today. Do you want to come along?"

"No, I was over there yesterday, and they are doing great. Sandy's mother is there, and everything seems to be under control. Sandy looks great."

"I can't wait to hold the baby if the 'grandma' will allow me to."

"She will. I got to hold him. He is a little bundle."

Julie stopped at Sandy and Mark's after work to see the baby.

"He is adorable. Marcus, you are a cutie! Can I hold him, Sandy?"

"Of course you can."

"Wow, it has been a long time since I have held a baby this small. It is awesome, and he smells so new."

Sandy introduced Julie to her mother, and she saw that Sandy looked a lot like her.

"It is nice to meet you. Thank you for letting me come over and see the baby. I know that you are getting back on your feet, Sandy, but I could not stay away much longer."

"It is great that you came, and we want you to stay for dinner. Mom made her great-tasting meatloaf. It is my comfort food and reminds me of home."

"I would love to, if you don't mind."

Julie noticed Mark just glowed the whole time. He was so proud of the baby. They were such a family now; they had come a long way, especially Sandy, from when they met. She did not think she could settle down, and yet she was so content and very happy. When Julie was on her way home, she got a call from George.

"Julie, I am ready to sell the house to you if you are interested."

"Yes, what is the price that you are asking?"

He quoted the price, and he said that he would include the furniture for $2,000 more. "I am including the furniture because then I would not have to haul it all out of there."

"I do appreciate that, George. Let me get back to you. I think I need to talk to my bank."

"Is the price too high?" George asked.

"No, not at all. I am thrilled! I just need to know with my bank when I can get the funds and the closing date. How soon do you want to close, George?"

"When it is good for you."

When they hung up, Julie was so excited. She couldn't believe it. According to the comps the realtor showed her, she'd gotten a great deal. She just did not know what to say to him. She was speechless. She thought, *I can't breathe. It's so great. Wow!* Julie called Thomas and told him about the deal with the house so he would not be setting up any more showings for her.

"That is incredible, Julie. You really did get a good deal for that area."

"I know! I hope he does not regret selling it to me at that price."

"I am sure he is making plenty of money on it, and remember, it releases him from renters and taxes."

"Thomas, I never thought about all of that. Maybe I should have offered him less money." They both laughed. George had said that he and his wife decided it was time to travel.

Beth was really busy at work this week and decided to go look at some apartments again. She wanted to live with Julie, but if that did not work out for her, she needed a place to go, and she should think about maybe living in her own place, which would be nice too. There were some that she looked at last week, but she really wanted to see more and at other locations. She wanted a pool for sure and a gym so she could work out, and those did not have all that she was looking for.

After work, Beth headed out to see some more apartments that she had looked up online at work. Beth thought, *I will stop at the one tonight and check out the other two this weekend.* Her phone started ringing, and it was Randy.

"Hi, Randy. How are you?"

"I am fine, and I just got back in town. I was hoping we could get together tomorrow night if you don't have any plans."

"I am going out with some friends Saturday night, but maybe we can get together on Sunday. I would like to see you."

"Okay, Sunday. Maybe we can take a drive and go to the fairgrounds and the flea market."

"Sounds like fun. I will look forward to that." Beth hung up and thought she would not be able to look at apartments. She would have to do it next week unless he wanted to look at a couple with her. That might work. She would ask him.

Julie was so excited and could not wait to tell Beth when she got home. Where was she anyway? There was so much that she had to do to this house. She would meet with the bank on Monday and get the process moving. She wouldn't tell the kids until after she went to the bank and get the loan. She would have to do an inspection, which maybe she would let slide unless the bank disapproved of that because George had really kept up on this place, and they have not had any problems since they lived there.

Beth came walking in the door, and Julie jumped to tell her the news.

Beth said, "Oh my, I am so excited for you and me! I was looking at apartments with no luck, and now I don't have to look. This is great news. What do you do now?"

"I have to go to the bank on Monday and get the loan processing, and then it should take about thirty days, according to the bank. The best part too is that George is letting me buy the furniture for a small price that I will include in the loan."

Beth said, "All the furniture! Wow! He must have read our minds. We love this furniture. It must be hard for him to give up his family home, though. I think it would be hard for me to do, saying goodbye to all the family memories."

"Yes, I think so. I think that is why it took him so long to get back to me about selling it. Well, I think I am going to the gym to work out to keep myself occupied because I can't stop thinking about it. I may take the day off Monday and get all this underway. I want to call my kids to tell them, but I want to wait until I get the loan processing so I can give them a definite date to close. They will be so excited, and they will have a home again."

Walking to the gym, Julie was thinking about Ken and how she missed him. He seemed so into her. She wished it all did not happen. It would be nice to call him and share the news, but again, it was over. She had to move on, and it was a great opportunity, a new house, and a great job. She thought of calling Diane when she got home and let her know that her idea turned out to be a reality. She wished she would move there. Diane said she was thinking about it if she could find a job there first. Hopefully that would come through soon, and she could stay with her until she found a place. Julie knew Diane would love it there.

After working out, she showered and had some lunch then called Diane. She was really happy for her and said she was going to call her. She decided to accept a position in Raleigh with an advertising company.

"Yay! That is wonderful. When will you start?"

"I am planning on being there in about three weeks if that is all right with you. I will need a place to stay."

Julie said, "I just can't tell you how much this means to me that you are moving here. Of course, you can stay with me for as long as you need to."

"Tell me more about the house situation. When will you know more?"

"I am going to the bank on Monday. It was too late to talk to them today. Diane, I can't keep thinking about Ken. I know that is crazy, but I miss him, and right away I wanted to call him about the house. I don't know why, but I just keep thinking about him and wish he was still a part of my life. Maybe I was wrong, and this is my conscience telling me just that. Maybe I judged the situation all wrong."

"I don't know what to tell you, Julie, other than maybe you should consider meeting with him and talking with him. He has been trying to do so after all."

"If he calls again, I will meet with him and talk."

CHAPTER 31

Sandy got up to get her baby boy—what a joy he was! He was just whimpering a little, but she wanted to see him. She picked him and fed him. She better let her mother sleep this morning since she would be leaving soon. She better get used to these early morning feedings herself. Mark was wonderful with the baby, but he had to go to work every day, so Sandy would be on her own, and she hoped she could handle this by herself. Her mom would be leaving on Sunday, and she would miss her help, but she couldn't stay forever, and she knew it would be hard for her to leave, but she needed to get back to work. She really liked Mark, and they got along well.

Sandy's life has changed so much in just months. She never wanted to get married and settle down, but she had ended up married with a baby, and she was really happy. Her life could not have turned out better. Mark got up and came over to look at her feeding the baby.

"Can I feed him?"

"Sure, sit down, and I will give him to you." Mark sat, and Sandy handed him the baby.

"You are such a natural with him, Mark. He does not seem to intimidate you at all."

"No, I really like holding him and being with him. He is my little guy. I can't wait until he gets bigger and we can play together."

"That is really sweet, Mark. It won't be long. They say they grow up so fast."

"I am enjoying this right now, and I love cuddling him all day. You're a good mom, Sandy. Who knew?"

She did not know herself, but she thought she was a good mom. Her mom got up, and they gave the baby a bath and put him back to bed. Mom said, "Now he will probably sleep until his next feeding. He is a good baby. Do you think you will be all right after I leave? I mean, are you ready for me to leave, or do you want me to stay longer?"

"No, you have been great, and I would like you to stay, but I need to learn to do this myself. I can't kidnap you for too long. I hope you come back soon to see us."

"Oh, I will. You won't be able to keep me away from seeing him grow."

"I will try to get home when he is a little bigger and Mark has some time off. I can't wait to show him off to my old friends. I bet they are surprised that I am married with a baby."

"They are. They said they never thought you would get married and settle down. You were always such a party girl."

"I never knew I would enjoy this better than partying, but I do. Well, it goes to show you never know what the future brings around."

"Sandy, you have definitely grown up."

CHAPTER 32

On Monday morning, Julie decided to take the day and go to the bank. She couldn't believe it was happening. She was so excited to have her very own place. She met with the loan officer, and he said that he would be starting the loan process and that we should close in thirty days.

"Wonderful, thank you, and let me know if you need anything else from me," I said. "I have decided that I am not going to have the house inspected because I have been living there, and George, the owner, has kept the place in immaculate condition."

"We will leave that up to your discretion, Julie."

She shook the loan officer's hand and left. On the way home, Julie started thinking of what she would need to do once the house was closed as far as the bedrooms: getting them ready for the kids and a room for Beth and for Diane when she got here. When Julie arrived at the house, she went in and looked all through the house and at all the rooms. *This is so surreal. This is going to be my place.* Looking at the bedrooms, she decided that Beth could use the room she was already using and that the guest room would work for Diane. Julie would stay in her bedroom, and Stephanie and Harry would have the other two bedrooms. There, that was easy. Everyone had a bedroom. She would still have the den if there was other company visiting. She thought, *Unbelievable. I love this house, and it is going to be mine, and I can't wait. I think I should have gone to work to keep myself busy, but I think I will just sit here and take it all in, enjoying my own excitement.*

Julie called George and told him that the loan officer had started the loan and they should close in thirty days. He was happy for that news and said to keep in touch if she needed anything. Thinking about calling the kids, Julie thought, *No, I better let this get a little closer to closing before I tell them.*

She decided, though, to call her mother and let her know the news. She was so happy for her. "Mom, you will have to come and visit. It would be great. I have a den that is all set up for you."

"I am really happy for you, and I will definitely do that as soon as you are settled, and then I can help you with things you may need done."

"You won't have to help me, Mom. Diane is moving to Raleigh and will be staying with me for a while, and of course, I have Beth here."

"Why are you not at work?" her mother asked.

"I needed to go to the bank, and thought I would be longer than I was, and so now I am too happy to concentrate on work. I may just go shop for groceries and make dinner tonight. Beth is really happy for me too, and she is going to stay here with me for a while. She is going to school, and this will help her not worry about getting a place. I enjoy her company, so that will be nice for both of us."

"Well, I am really happy for you, Julie, and I will talk to you again soon."

After speaking to her mother, Julie headed to the grocery store. As she was checking out, someone came up behind her. It was Ken.

"How are you, Julie?"

Shocked to see him, Julie gasped, not knowing what to do or say. "I am fine, and you?"

"I am doing well, and I still miss you. I want you to know that. What are you doing now?"

"I am heading home. Why don't you come over? I have to unload my groceries, and we can talk."

"I would like that. I will follow you home."

Julie and Ken entered the house. He helped her with the groceries, and she started to unpack. Things felt a bit awkward, and Julie said, "Can I get you a soda or a glass of wine?"

"Yes, thanks. Wine sounds nice."

"I think wine sounds right for me right now too. I have been thinking that we started seeing each other too soon. Maybe we were not ready for a relationship with each other."

"No, I am ready for a relationship, and I knew that as soon as I met you, Julie. I fell for you the minute I saw you in the club. I felt it right there, seeing you. I had a feeling inside me that you were the one, and I know that may sound crazy, but that is how I felt, and I still feel that way. Just give me another chance."

"I have been wanting to call you. I felt the same way when I met you. But you crushed me and made me feel so insecure and questioning myself and my feelings. I am just scared because of that night that maybe you wanted someone better than me. Tell me what were you doing that night. What were you thinking, and what were you doing? You need to think very carefully how you answer that question because everyone there that night saw it and thought the same thing. My friends and my daughter, that really hurt me, you know. So tell me, Ken, what were you doing?" Julie could feel the quiver in her voice, and her eyes started to tear up. She was afraid of what Ken was going to say.

"I wasn't doing anything. I had never been in that situation before when someone stuck to my hip. I did not want to be rude, so I just let it happen. I never was leading into anything with her."

Julie looked at his handsome face as he started to blush, and she could see his hands were shaking. She just wanted to go and hug him so badly, but she listened intently to what he was going to say.

"I was being friendly for you and the others, knowing it was your party and your friends. I had no idea that it looked the way you all interpreted it to be."

"Then what gave her the impression that you were interested in her?"

"I don't know what she was thinking or what her thoughts were. I can't be guilty for what she thought. I gave her no reason to believe that I was interested in her," Ken said.

"She told Beth you told her that you wanted to see her again." *He just keeps lying,* thought Julie. "Have you ever contacted her, or has she contacted you since that night?" Julie asked.

"No, I have not heard from her or contacted her, nor have I wanted to."

"So you are telling me that I have been wrong and all my friends have been wrong?"

"Yes, that is the way it is, and I can't believe that you would not believe me and that you thought I would do something like that right in front of you. I want to be in a committed relationship. That is who I am, and you knowing the reason I left my wife should confirm that about me. I would not want anyone to go through the pain I went through, nor would I put anyone through that kind of nonsense. I want to make this right with you, Julie, if you would please give me another chance."

"I can't, Ken. I could never believe another word you say to me, ever. I can't make another mistake in my life like the twenty years with my ex. Life is too short."

Ken looked shocked, and his face was turning a faded gray, and he said, "I thought we could work this out, and I am sorry. I wish that night never happened. I will not put you through any more grief, Julie. I will say goodbye."

He left, and Julie just stood there. She could not even take a breath thinking of how this relationship went so wrong. He should have never done it to her, and he would never do it again.

When Beth got home, Julie had dinner on the table, and she was so impressed since she was not the one who liked to cook. She actually liked dinner. They poured a glass of wine and went outside on the porch.

"I saw Ken today."

"You did what? Finally, what took you so long to call him?"

"I did not call him. I ran into him today at the store, and he followed me home, and we talked."

Beth said, "I am so glad. Are you two getting back together?"

"No, Beth. We are not back together. The relationship is over with Ken, and I would never take him back. I would be a fool. I know he was lying to me, so that shows that he has no respect or consideration for me."

"Julie, I am sorry, and I know how you must be feeling. I think you did the right thing, though I know it had to be hard for you."

"You know, Beth, fool me once, but you can't fool me twice, and I actually feel better now, almost relieved, so that I can move on."

CHAPTER 33

Beth was thinking about her date with Randy that weekend. He was nice, but Beth was not sure that she wanted to get too attached. She needed to focus on school, but she would keep dating him since he was nice to be around. She went up to her room and started to study a little more. After logging on to her computer, she signed in and was ready to go with her school assignment. After she finished her assignment, she called Sandy to tell her about Julie and Ken.

"I don't know if Julie called you, but her and Ken have met and talked today, and it is completely over between the two. They are no longer going to be a couple. It seems that we did not jump to a conclusion. We were right about what we saw him doing. Julie was not going to have any more of it from Ken. I feel bad about that, and I know how much she cared about him, but I am so glad that she is moving on without him. You may want to give her a call, Sandy. She may want to talk about this more with you. I think the more she talks to everybody about it, she will have it confirmed in her mind and will start over faster."

"You're right, Beth. Thanks. I will give her a call," said Sandy.

Sandy called Julie and invited her to go out for dinner tomorrow night. "I am going to bring the baby too. I feel like getting out of the house."

"I can't wait to see you. I have something to tell you," Julie said.

"I know what you are going to say," Sandy said. "Beth told me you and Ken are finished."

"Sandy, I could not take him back. However, I really wanted to, but this is the best thing for me, though I wasted all that time with him, and now I can move on."

"I'm sorry, Julie."

"No, that's okay. I feel relieved that I made the right decision and let go of the pain I have been feeling."

"I know you, Julie. You have a lot going for you, and I know you will be okay. Life can take us through so many twists and turns," said Sandy.

Julie thought, *How crazy. This is Sandy, who said she would never trust a man, and here she is married with a baby, and her life just seems perfect right now. I hope that continues for them, and they have many more babies.*

Sandy said, "I never thought I could be this happy, but I am so in love with Mark, and I know that we are going to continue to have a good life together. Every day I enjoy waking up to him and the baby. I am not saying this to make you feel bad but letting you know that there will be a relationship that will work out for you too. I want to give you hope."

"Thank you, Sandy. You know, I have been seeing Thomas, my realtor. You should see him. He is gorgeous, but I am not jumping forward with him just yet. Right now

I just want to buy this house and live my own life. Did Beth tell you that she is going to stay here with me?" Julie asked.

"Yes, she did. That is great for both of you."

"I have not told the kids about the house yet."

"Why, don't you want to tell them?" asked Sandy.

"I just want to be sure there are no problems getting the mortgage. There should not be a problem, but you never know. I want to be sure everything is secure first. I don't want to jinx it, as they say. One thing, I don't have to pack anything. That is such a big positive for me and for Beth."

"Are you going to change anything about the house, Julie?" asked Sandy.

"I don't know yet. I am still thinking about maybe painting and getting new pictures for the walls and just personalizing it to my taste, but nothing major, I don't think. I have a lot of antiques that I can finally put out."

"Mark and I are thinking about buying a single-family home too."

"You are?"

"I really like the place we have now. It has plenty of space, so we are not going to rush into it, but a single-family rather than a condo would be nice, to have a private backyard for the baby, but we don't need that just yet either. I better get back to the baby, and I will see you tomorrow evening."

"When you are ready, I know a really good realtor I can refer you to," Julie said and laughed.

"Mark, it seems that Julie is still seeing Thomas. I think we should have them over for drinks some night and maybe dinner. Since we don't get to go out too often, we should have people in more. They are going to the beach this weekend, and so maybe next weekend I will give them a call."

"I am on your side with that. We need to keep up our social life even though we have our little guy," Mark said.

"I had a really good time having dinner with the girls. We talked and laughed. They gloated over Marcus, and it was like old times. I am so excited for Julie getting the house as it is, furniture and all, which is amazing."

"Why is he including all the furniture, Sandy?" Mark asked.

"He told Julie he would have to sell it anyway, and this way he does not have to rent a truck to transfer it somewhere to be sold. So Julie really makes out because that furniture is still in really nice shape. She won't have to buy anything for a while unless she wants to. Thinking about that…I am terrible working for other people. I think that I should think about starting my own business, and I was thinking a flower shop."

"Really, Sandy, when did you have the time to think about something like that?" Mark asked.

"Well, I love flowers, and that is something that I can order, rather than growing them, and open a little shop to get started."

"What about the baby?"

"Not right now, but I just want us to think about that as a possibility for me."

"I like the idea. I really do. It would suit you just fine. We can look around at some commercial property for the costs and then start budgeting for it," Mark said.

"That is exciting! Thank you for allowing me to dream, Mark."

"It is not just a dream but a big possibility for you, and I like the plan. I will be behind you 100 percent."

CHAPTER 34

"The beach is beautiful," Julie said.

"I am glad that you agreed to come with me this weekend," Thomas said. "The weather will be starting to change a little now, and it is not as crowded, so this is when you can really appreciate the beach."

I still can't believe I am here with this gorgeous man, thought Julie. *Someone better pinch me.*

They walked the beach and watched the high waves rolling to shore. Julie looked at Thomas and held his strong hand as they walked and collected seashells and sat and watched the waves come in; it was very romantic. They could not stop looking at each other. They did not say a word, but they knew they enjoyed each other's company. Sometimes it's better not to say a word, just feel the closeness. Thomas stopped walking. He held her and gave her a warm kiss and hug, and they continued walking the beach.

That night they tried a new restaurant with a huge variety of seafood to choose from. The weather was warm and calm, so they sat outside at the bar while they waited for their table. While they were having a drink and waiting for their table, they met another couple, and they asked them to join them for a drink. They were from New Jersey originally and had recently moved to the coast.

They said they had always vacationed here in the summer when their kids were young and really loved it and the weather. The group had a great conversation going, so they asked Julie and Thomas to join them for dinner. They were very nice, and they had a great visit with them. Julie told them as they parted to call and come to Raleigh for a visit, and they said yes and to keep in touch and come visit them. They exchanged phone numbers and email addresses.

Julie looked at Thomas and said, "What an interesting couple. I think that we just made some new friends, and they live at the coast. It will be nice to visit them when we come down again."

"Wow! That's nice, Julie, that you said when we come back to the beach together again. I like that."

The next day, they stayed in the hotel most of the day making passionate love, and it was amazing enjoying each other intensely. Julie thought, *Thomas is an incredible lover, and I have to say the best I have ever had.* Later, they went to the beach and sat out the rest of the day until after dark, all alone with the waves hitting the shore and the sun setting in the sky. The next day, they were sad, as they had to pack and start back home.

CHAPTER 35

On Wednesday morning, Julie's phone rang. It was the loan officer.

"Hi, Julie. We are ready for a closing date on your house, and your loan has been approved. Will two weeks work for you?" Julie started jumping, and her heart was pounding. It was finally happening!

"Thank you! I am so happy about this! I will see you then."

After hanging up the phone, Julie called Thomas and told him the good news. Then she called her son and daughter and told them. They were really happy for her and for themselves to have a home to come home to. Feeling very satisfied with herself, Julie poured a glass of wine to calm her nerves. This was terrific! Thomas said he would be over later, and they would go to dinner to celebrate.

When Thomas arrived, she was still bouncing around with excitement. She gave him a big hug and said that she was just so excited that she couldn't calm down.

"Well," he said, "let's go to dinner and have a cocktail, and that should help us celebrate this great news."

"I am so happy, Thomas. This feels like an accomplishment. Nothing like this has happened to me before. It's like getting your degree from college. You have accomplished something big that is going stay with you all your life."

"I am really happy for you, Julie. I just hope you get that excited and over me," Thomas said, and he laughed.

"Of course I do. You know that you are the best, and you mean so much to me. This is just, you know, different. This is like my very own accomplishment. It is not a love affair, or maybe it is."

She laughed. One thing between Thomas and her was taking this relationship day to day with no expectations; however, there was definitely so much going on between them.

"After dinner, we should go over to Sandy and Mark's and tell them. I already told Beth," Julie said.

After dinner, they stopped at Sandy and Mark's. They were surprised to see them, and when they entered, the baby was fussing, and they looked a little stressed. Julie took the baby and rocked him, and he hushed for a while. She told them about the house, and they were very happy for her. Thomas and Julie did not stay long. They left and went back to the house.

"Thomas, do you think should I change anything about the house?"

"No, why would you? It looks great, and I can't believe he included the furniture into the house price because it is really nice furniture," Thomas said.

"I know. I could not believe it either. It is all mine. Maybe sometime down the road after the New Year, I will give it a fresh coat of paint."

They had a glass of wine and went up to the bedroom and celebrated some more in a very intimate way. Julie knew Thomas really liked her energy. She was also thinking that maybe someday it would be their bedroom together, but she did not say a word.

CHAPTER 36

The weeks had passed, and Julie was now a homeowner. The kids were coming home for the weekend, and her mother was flying in. Julie would be picking her up at the airport, and she couldn't wait to see her. She asked Thomas to join them for dinner on Saturday evening. She thought it would be nice for her mother to meet him. She knew that she was going to like him. Julie had told her so much about him; she should feel as though she already knew him.

Beth was anxious to meet her mother too. She was going to live with her for a while. She would not want it any other way. Julie and Beth had gotten really close. Beth could stay as long as she wanted. She was going out with her friends, and Julie thought she was doing that so she would have time with her family.

Julie would have Sandy and Mark come over for dessert later in the evening. She just wanted to have some time with her kids and mother before they all came over, and Beth should be back from visiting her friends by then too. It might just be overwhelming for her mother, seeing the house and meeting Julie's friends all at once. She did not want to overwhelm her. She would be staying for the whole week. She was so happy that she would have some time with her. Diane was supposed to arrive too but would be delayed a week because of finishing up some loose ends on her job.

Beth was looking forward to meeting Julie's mother. It would be nice to have her company around. Julie had been so happy since she had gotten together with Thomas. They really looked good together, and she was ecstatic, of course, buying this house. Beth loved the house, and she was so glad Julie was letting her stay and pay her rent. They had become such great friends, and she felt that way about her kids too. They were all like family.

Beth met a new guy, and she might invite him over after dinner. She wanted to get Julie's thoughts about him. His name was Bill, and she really liked spending time with him. She had not even mentioned him to Julie because she had been so busy and had been spending so much time with Thomas. Beth just never brought it up to her. She might be a little shocked that she did not share that with her, but she knew she would get over it.

Bill had had Beth over to his place for dinner, and he was a great cook. They both liked to cook, and that was amazing to have that in common. They mostly hang out there at his place. They didn't go out too much. He was just finishing up his master's degree, so they had that in common also.

They did go to a party at his friend's house; it was a little wild, and everyone was drunk. One of his friends cornered Beth in the restroom and kept trying to put his hand all over her and kiss her until Bill came to the rescue. That was awkward and embarrassing to her that it was one of his friends. Beth had one wife get mad because her husband kept flirting with her, which was outrageous. She told Beth that she should leave and gave her a look that could kill.

"Bill, I don't think I like your friends. I am sorry to say that, but it is obvious that they all have some issues. Am I wrong about this?"

He said, "No, they do have issues. They are all insecure, and I think they have never grown up."

"Why do you hang out with them then? They really don't seem like your type of people."

"I know. I try not to spend so much time with them. I have known them for so long and their craziness since my early college days, but I do know that I need to move on from them. I am sorry. I should not have brought you here. I should have known that they would get drunk and rowdy. I hope you won't judge me because of the company I keep."

"I think I am having second thoughts right now," Beth said and laughed.

CHAPTER 37

When Mark got home, Sandy told him that she was looking forward to going to Julie's and meeting her mother and showing off their baby.

"That was nice of her to invite us over. I will fix an appetizer to take over, something that will not be too heavy since they will be having dinner before we get there. I don't know why she did not invite us for dinner too."

Mark said, "How long will we be staying there, because I am really tired tonight? Working on a Saturday was just overwhelming today."

"You sound a little grumpy today. What is wrong?" Sandy asked.

"It is work. They expect too much, and I am not happy. You know how there are certain someones that you just can't work with," Mark said.

"Yes, I do know what you mean. I still feel bad about being let go from there. I won't say fired. I am just not good working with people, especially supervisors. I really need to find my own work like the flower shop we discussed."

"Whatever you decide, Sandy, I will be supporting you."

She looked at him and said, "You are great, and I am so glad that I married you." She gave him a big hug and kiss.

"Sandy, you have been looking tired lately. Are you getting enough sleep?"

"I have finally been able to sleep all night long since the baby, so maybe I am getting too much sleep, and my body does not know how to process that just yet." She laughed. "I have been feeling a little tired lately, though."

Mark said, "It has been a while since there has not been any crying through the night. Maybe he will sleep awhile now so we can have a get-together. Why don't you follow grumpy me into my cave?" They both walked happily into the bedroom with smiles on their faces.

"We do have a party to go to, you know," she said as she closed the door.

CHAPTER 38

When Julie's mother entered the house, she was overwhelmed. Julie gave her a tour around the house.

"This is beautiful, and it is more house than what I thought it would be. It is so big, and it has so much character. Oh my, how are you going to manage all of this?"

"I will be fine, Mother. I want you to come and stay with me as long as you want. There is plenty of room for you and Dad. Remember I told you that Beth is going to stay, and of course, the kids will be home when school is over in the summer. They will not be taking summer classes this next year. Harry will be able to help me with some of the outside, cutting grass, and other chores. Let's talk about us. I miss our shopping trips. Going to the mall and having lunch or dinner, it was always our time together. It was great."

"Well, I am here now, finally, and we can do those things. I miss getting your advice on how to dress, and I miss my best friend to talk to in person." They hugged.

"Why don't you go unpack and take a shower and relax? The kids will be here shortly, and they will be happy to see you and will probably talk your ear off, so prepare yourself. I can't wait to introduce you to Thomas. I know you will like him. I am going to start putting dinner together and get organized in the kitchen."

"I think I will take a little nap then shower, and then I will come down and help you get dinner ready," her mother said.

"Okay, see you in a little while."

It is so nice she is here, thought Julie. *I wish she could stay. Maybe I should suggest she and Dad to move here too and stay with me. They would both love the weather. It is much warmer than Connecticut. I'm excited that Diane is coming here and will be staying awhile until she gets settled into her new job.*

"Mom did I tell you that Diane is going to stay with me when she moves here until she gets settled in?"

"No, I don't think you told me that she made it a permanent decision."

"Yes, she did when she came to visit. She really liked it here, and she sold her house and found a job. Anytime you want to move here with me, you and Dad just let me know. I would love to have you."

"Thanks, Julie, but we have the house and all my friends and church. I think I should just stay put for now. I think you have your hands full right now with your kids, Beth, and Diane moving in."

"Beth and Diane are only going to be temporary. Diane has a job, so once she gets settled, she will find a place of her own. Beth will also eventually move out. She just wants to get through school. Let's go shopping this week and get Stephanie and Harry some new bedding for their rooms. What do you think?"

"That sounds like a plan," she said.

"I need to personalize this house to us."

The doorbell rang, and it was Stephanie and Harry. Julie said, "This is our house. You don't have to ring the doorbell. You just come in."

"Yeah," Stephanie said. "That sounds so nice to me. This is home. This is great, Mom. I am so happy for you for buying this home. I liked it the first time I saw it, and it is amazing that it is yours or ours. It feels nice to have real home again. Hi, Grandma, it is nice to see you."

"I am happy to be here, and you two look wonderful. All that college intellectual information must be good for both of you." Harry smiled and laughed.

"Take your suitcases upstairs while we are getting dinner ready. You can go into the living room and visit while I get this together."

"Why don't I help you get dinner together, and the kids and I can always talk over dinner or later?" Mother asked.

"Okay, I just thought you might want to sit and relax. It has been a long day for you, but I could use your help. Thanks." Julie figured that maybe she was a little nervous too and needed to keep busy.

Thomas showed up with flowers for Julie's mother, which was very thoughtful, and she was very impressed with that. They all went into the living room and talked until dinner was ready. They sat around the dinner table talking; they all had so much to catch up on, and they did. The conversations just flowed. Stephanie told everyone that she had been dating someone that she would like us to meet.

Harry said, "I have also been seeing someone special that I really like, but I'm not ready for everyone to meet just yet." They laughed at that.

"With Christmas around the corner, maybe we will all be ready for introductions then," Julie said.

"That may be possible. We'll see," said Harry.

After dinner, they cleared the table, and Julie told them Beth should be on her way home and that Sandy and Mark were coming over with the baby.

When Sandy and Mark arrived with the baby, everyone was taken by him. Sandy explained that he was a little fussy since it was getting near his bedtime. Beth arrived shortly after, and it was nice for my mother to meet them all. Julie held the baby and let Sandy and Mark relax a little and enjoy their dessert. Julie thought it would be nice to get the dessert out immediately since the baby was a little fussy.

"It is overwhelming at times," Sandy said. "He gets into his fussy stage, and there is little you can do with him but hold him."

Mark said, "It is really making us a little tired and grumpy."

Sandy said, "Are you saying I am grumpy?"

Julie thought it must be hormones because she did seem a little grumpy, but that was understandable.

"No," Mark said, "that is me included. I am tired, and when I am tired, like a baby, I get grumpy."

"Okay then, I will give you that. I just don't want you telling everyone that it is me." They gave each other a hug.

Beth said, "I did not realize how much is involved with having a baby. It sounds like it really changes your routine a lot."

"It does," Julie's mother said. "It is a very trying time when they are this little, but it will get better for both of you soon."

"I am glad to hear it," said Mark. "It is very trying. I will agree."

"I never had kids," Thomas said. "I could only imagine what it would be like."

Julie felt a little sad right then, never giving it a thought that maybe Thomas would like kids of his own. *The problem is it would not be with me. That time is long gone. I wonder if he will regret that,* she thought.

Stephanie said, "One day I want to have at least two kids."

Harry said, "At least one."

"Great," Julie said. "I will look forward to grandchildren but not too soon. I am too young to be a grandma. No time soon, you two." Everyone laughed.

Sandy said, "Believe me. You will have plenty of time in the future."

Julie looked at Thomas to see what his reaction was to those statements, but he did not seem to be bothered at all.

After everyone had left, the kids and Julie's mother went to bed, and Julie and Thomas sat there talking about the evening.

"I think my mother really likes you."

"It must have been the flowers," he said, and they laughed.

"When we were talking about the baby, I was thinking that we never really talked about kids. I have two, but what about you?"

"What do you mean?" Thomas asked.

"Do you feel that you will regret never having any children of your own?"

"Really, that is something I never ever considered. There is something that I really need to tell you, and that is that I can't have children. I found that out when I was first married, and we were thinking about having children like newlyweds do. I should have told you. I am sorry. Neither my ex-wife nor I really cared about having any children. For one thing, I think she was just too into herself to have to share it with anyone, including kids and me or anyone for that matter. So at that time it was for the better, and since then I just got over it and never really thought about it again. But I do enjoy being around children, and I especially like yours. They are great kids."

"I am sorry you can't have children of your own. You would be a great father. I know that must have been a terrible blow. I am glad that it does not bother you. Well, we have grandchildren to look forward to someday." Julie's face turned beet red. "I am sorry. I should not have said that. It is inappropriate. That is, if we get married someday, that is what I am thinking."

"That is what I am thinking too, and I do want to make it a reality. I wonder because you just bought this house and want to move on with your accomplishments if that will include me," Thomas asked.

"Of course it will. I want to you to be with me always, now and in the future," Julie said.

"I am so glad to hear that," Thomas said, and they held each other tight.

On the way home, Sandy looked at Mark. "I had a good time. It was so nice to get out. However, I can't wait to get to bed. I am exhausted."

"I will put Marcus to bed, Sandy. You go ahead and climb into bed, and I will join you shortly."

The baby must have known that Mark and Sandy were exhausted because he slept through the night. Thinking that she had not been feeling well lately and she had missed her period, she decided to call the doctor and see what was up. It just might be a hormone thing going on. She made the appointment to see the doctor next week.

CHAPTER 39

Leaving the doctor's office, Sandy was so relieved to know that it was only her crazy hormones and a bit of exhaustion from having Marcus. She thought, *I can't wait to tell Mark. I hope he won't be disappointed. I think he thought I was pregnant again.* She picked Marcus from the babysitters and headed to the store. She thought she would put some steaks on the grill and have a salad for dinner. Mark always enjoyed steaks.

Sandy decided to call her mother and see if she would be able to come back again and stay a couple of days. She and Mark could really use the break, maybe even get away a day or two. She did tell her to call if they needed anything, and since the doctor told her to try to get more rest, it would be a great time for her to come. Sandy knew her mother missed them and wanted to see Marcus. She would give her a call tomorrow. She wanted to talk to Mark about it first.

It was almost Christmas, and Sandy had not bought the baby or Mark anything for Christmas. She needed to go shopping. She could take Marcus with her; he wouldn't know the difference of what he saw when she put it under the tree. He was still our little baby. They would be spending Thanksgiving at Julie's, and maybe her mother would come up that Thanksgiving weekend. She liked to get her shopping done early before the Christmas rush, and after Thanksgiving, they could put up the tree.

Bill and Beth were a couple now. They had so much in common; they had both gotten their MBAs and gotten promoted at their jobs. How rare was that? Beth had never heard from Randy again. It was like he evaporated into thin air, which had worked out for the best for Bill and her getting together.

They had taken up canoeing and gone to the beach often. They didn't see his old crazy friends anymore. They had made a lot of new friends and got invited out onto their boats quite often. Bill wanted Beth to meet his parents during Christmas, and she was wondering why, although it would be good to see what they were like and if they would approve of her. She better get ready.

Bill would be there shortly. They were meeting up with some friends downtown, so she better put on makeup, finish dressing, and put on some perfume. The doorbell rang, and it was Bill.

"You are early. I am not ready yet," Beth said.

"That's okay. I'll wait. I just wanted to make sure we are not late. We will have to find parking, and it is Saturday night, you know!"

He looked really good with his dark hair and eyes and always seemed to be dressed just right. *I am beginning to think he is a neat freak. I like being with him. His personality is just so sweet and boyish all the time,* Beth thought. "Okay, Bill. I will be down in about ten minutes."

CHAPTER 40

Julie was thinking that Thanksgiving was so nice this year, and again, Christmas was just around the corner. She had shopping to finish and a tree to put up. She better get busy decorating too. It was her first official Christmas in the house that she bought all by herself. That was just so fabulous for her to accomplish.

Diane had been working a lot lately and dating. She met a nice guy at work. She really liked it here in Raleigh, and Julie thought she looked so happy and even a little younger. It had been so nice having her there, but she found a house. She was looking into buying with Thomas's help. It was going to get really quiet around there.

Beth was gone most of the time. She was always at the beach boating or canoeing with Bill. She just got back from visiting her parents at Thanksgiving. Julie was sure she told them about Bill. There were times Julie thought she would like to move back home. She missed her family.

Julie had not heard from Ken in a long time. He had finally stopped calling her. He was hurt, but it was far more hurtful to her. She thought he was going to be her soul mate, but he was actually just a waste of my time. Thomas had been a godsend. He was busy with his real estate firm, but they always took time for each other. They had taken many getaway trips together to other countries. Julie never thought she would go out of the country, and they had taken cruises together; it had been wonderful. She had gone to his parties for work, and they went to the beach often. The kids just loved him.

Julie thought that the reason it was working for them was that there had been no expectations in their relationship from each other; they just went day to day the way they wanted to. However, they were inseparable.

CHAPTER 41

It had been one year since Julie bought her first house, and she still loved it. The kids were in their last year of school and would soon be looking for employment. They were both so ready to get out of school and get on with their lives.

Beth and Bill had moved in together about six months ago and were very happy and were planning on getting engaged.

Mark and Sandy sold the condo and bought a house only a couple of blocks from Julie's house. Marcus had really grown, and they were expecting their second child.

Thomas and Julie had been married a year now. He asked her to marry him last Christmas, and they married shortly after. It was a small wedding in a chapel. Since they were both married before, they did not need anything big. Julie was so happy to be married to a gorgeous man and her forever soul mate.

They had never forgotten Mary, and they always talked about what her possibilities would have been if she would have lived. Her boyfriend, James Brody, would be spending the rest of his life in jail and would never hurt anyone again.

Beth, Sandy, and Julie never spent a holiday without being together. They were all happy, and their lives had turned out to be more than what they even expected when they arrived at the house just a few years ago. It had been a long road, but they had finally made it to new beginnings.

CPSIA information can be obtained
at www.ICGtesting.com
Printed in the USA
LVHW020735181121
703571LV00021B/1399

9 781638 378556